SILVER BELLS AND MISTLETOE

ANNA ST. CLAIRE

DEDICATION & REMEMBRANCE

For my sister, Susan, who always dreamed a hero would sweep her off her feet and treat her with the love that our storybooks foretell. I wish you all the happiness-ever-after that life can give.

And in remembrance of my sweet kitty, Noel. She was a Christmas gift from my daughter, and she kept us company for over nineteen years. Rest well, sweet Noel. You inspired parts of this story and are featured on the cover. We miss you.

Silver Bells and Mistletoe
By Anna St. Claire

Sassy Romances

CHAPTER 1

ate November 1819.
Brighton, England

Lady Susan Winslow stopped in mid-step and leaned over the top of the oaken bannister, straining to catch the conversation going on behind the closed doors to her father's library. Loud, angry voices bandied her name beyond the walls of the room, along with other words like *betrothal* and *earl*—words which directly concerned *her*. When the volume lowered, she hugged the wall and crept slowly down the stairs, desperate to hear more while trying not to be caught.

"So, *it is done*? You did not discuss this latest arrangement with me." Susan recognized her stepmother's shrill voice. She had two tones—shrill or whining. Susan hated both.

She spotted the large potted palm tree beside the door of the library, and with a wary glance around, scuttled behind it on tiptoe, the better to hear what was being said.

"Prucilla, I have listened to you already on this matter—

several times, in fact. I fear you do not have Susan's best interests at heart." Her father's voice was steady with an underlying hardness. He sounded angry.

"I see how it is going to be. You let her wind you about her little finger. Ha! She needs a husband who will take her in hand. Trust me, James, I know what a woman needs at her age. For months now I have been suggesting you seek a betrothal for her, and you have ignored all of my pleas until this one. What makes *this one* so special?"

"The betrothal is done. And so is this conversation."

Glass smashed against a wall, echoing off the dark mahogany paneled hallway where Susan hid. The door crashed open, barely missing the plant, and then her step-mother turned and slammed it shut behind her. Susan ducked. The angry woman stormed up the stairs. When Prucilla was out of sight, Susan tiptoed from behind the plant, opened the door and faced her father.

"Daughter, what are you doing here?"

"Papa why were you arguing about *me?*" she demanded without preamble. She searched his face for some sort of denial, anything to tell her she had heard wrong, but he just sat there behind his desk. "I heard you. What have you done?"

"I am sorry you overheard, although as the proverb says, 'eavesdroppers never hear good of themselves,'" he said sternly. "The news should have come from me. We need to talk."

"I beg your pardon… *what?* What should have come from you?" She bit her bottom lip and tasted the metallic flavour of her own blood, guiltily aware of her tone and her temper, and trying to control both. "Did you sign my life away? Did you sign betrothal papers?"

Her father stared for a moment, and then he smiled.

"Why are you smiling, Papa? I do not understand."

"Yes, daughter. You are betrothed or will be by the week's end."

"No. You cannot. Please, Papa, you promised. Let me have one Season... just one. If I do not find a match..."

He cut her off. "Be easy, daughter. You no longer need a Season. A good man has asked for your hand. I approve of him. You will be protected and be able to enjoy the life to which you are accustomed. You will be a countess. Trust me." He looked at her; his eyes seemed to implore her.

She could not speak. "Our men of business have already settled the details, and all that is required are the signatures," he continued.

"Why am I being given no choice in my intended spouse? You and Mama were a love-match. You have always told me I must follow my heart. But now you are forcing me to marry for position—or maybe it is because Prucilla wants to be rid of me."

"No. That is not *at all* the case." He reached for her hand, and she pulled it back.

Angry, Susan stared hopelessly around the room. A shelf of her own books came into view; stories which had helped her dream of her own life and the possibilities. She let out a cynical laugh.

"I have agreed to a betrothal. He approached me and I could find no reason to disagree. You are to be betrothed to an earl. We have agreed to the details and the papers are being signed."

"So, *my* life has to change because some horrid, grumpy old earl is ready to marry, and his fancy has alighted on me."

"Daughter. I want what is best for you."

"Please, Papa. Do not do this. You can change your mind and allow me my Season. I want to marry for love, as you did. I want a wedding like Mama would have planned for me.

Please give me a chance to want to marry a man I care about, Papa."

"Susan, try to see the good in this…"

"*Good?*" Her voice rose. "*Please*, Papa. *Do not* tell me you are doing this for my good."

"Susan, I am signing the betrothal papers. It is as good as done." Her papa's voice was firm. He had decided, and there was no reasoning with him.

The dark paneled walls of the library oppressed her. "You lied to me! Even if you sign the papers and drag me to the altar, I will never say the vows, and I will never acknowledge a husband." Throwing her hands over her ears, she kicked the brown leather chair in front of her and limped in pain from the room.

Oh, no. I think I have broken my toe. So much for making a grand exit. *Yet I meant everything I said.* She ignored the pain and fled from the house, needing air and time to reflect.

She ran to the stables and flung herself into her horse's stall. Smudge stood still, nudging her with his nose, already wet from her own tears. She must leave; go somewhere, do anything. She had just been given away to a life without love or choice. Livid, she felt an uncontrollable urge to run away and only became angrier when she remembered having spent her pin-money. Suddenly, she thought of her mother, gone now for over six years. Mama would find something to do and take her mind off this horrible episode. She drew herself up, kissed Smudge, and left the stable.

Hours later, the carriage stuffed with parcels paid for with her father's credit, Susan gazed from the window as the horses approached her family's small cemetery. The vehicle slowed down and inched alongside the graveyard, crunching the loose gravel near the front entrance, finally coming to a stop under a large walnut tree. The tall trunk supported knotty, barren branches with a span well beyond the width of the carriage.

"We should trim those. I must tell the gardener." She spoke absently, more to herself than to her half-asleep companion seated across from her. A small copse of trees which hugged the rear aspect of the fencing framed the family burial site, thus according a sense of privacy to those who rested here. The site used to be next to the old house and chapel, but when the wooden structure had caught fire, they built a newer brick house closer to the centre of the estate. The Winslow property, Satterfield Hall, was expansive, but it took fifteen minutes by carriage to get here.

Susan preferred to ride Smudge here, but the day had flown by. A bright orange sun was already dropping behind swiftly moving dark clouds and a hazy full moon was showing itself.

As the carriage slowed, her companion stirred.

"M'lady, 'tis getting late and there be a storm coming. It cannot feel right in my bones, our being here." Her abigail, Rose, looked around and, with an exaggerated gasp, pointed upwards at a large branch that covered the corner of the graveyard. "A crow," she squealed, "that is a sign of death."

As if he knew he was being singled out, the large black crow called out. "Caw... cawww... caw... cawwww!"

"Do not be silly, Rose." Susan shook her head, smiling. "This is a *graveyard. Of course*, there is death." Susan was aware Rose did not enjoy being out past four o'clock. She was superstitious and often cited superstitions to make situations more difficult. But Rose had been her own dear mother's lady's maid and now was hers, and even though Susan often found herself irritated with the woman, she could not entertain having a different maid.

Despite the admonishment she had just delivered to Rose,

Susan shuddered inside with her own sudden sense of fore-boding and tried to shake it off.

"Rose, I do not wish to be at outs with you. We are here, now. *You know* how important these visits are to me. The sun is still out…"

"Barely," her lady's maid interrupted, clearly in a huff.

"Yes, well, humour me, Rose. I want to spend time with my mother." She swallowed past the lump forming in her throat. "If anything were to threaten us, Daniel and Isaac are here, at the carriage, and will see." She gave a casual wave towards the front of the coach. "They will come to our aid." Susan closed her eyes and took a deep breath, letting it out slowly, an exercise she repeated whenever she felt cross. It kept her from saying something she could not take back. *Rose could irritate a saint. She is far too familiar.*

"As you say, m'lady," the old woman quipped as she glanced warily upwards. She muttered some sort of prayer under her breath, but when no reaction was forthcoming, grunted acceptance and tightened her black shawl around her shoulders.

The two women exited the sleek, black carriage, and walked through a narrow iron gate and down a small stone path that led to her mother's grave. Susan heard something fall from the tree and hastily looked around. A quickly moving cloud cast an enormous shadow, drawing her attention up to a threatening sky, and she urged Rose towards her mother's burial site. She marvelled at the speed that the slightly stooped, greying woman could move.

Susan looked back at the coach. It still stood under the wild walnut tree. Her family's crest was normally prominent, but on this occasion, thick, bare branches obscured it. Some might consider a walnut tree an odd choice for a cemetery—considering it bore fruit to pick—but her grandfather had planted it many years ago for the shade it offered during the warm months.

Her mother's final resting place stood in front of her. Its tall marble headstone lay next to a small iron bench, both framed by neatly tended red and white rose bushes. A large white marble dove perched protectively at the top of the headstone. Kneeling down, Susan brushed away the remnants of dead twigs and leaves. Small wind bursts picked up the fallen leaves and empty nutshells, swirling and flinging them against the fence and monuments. She smelled the graveside roses, and immediately felt closer to her mother.

"If you do not mind, m'lady, I would like to sit here a spell, just long enough to take the weight off my poor feet." Rose nodded at the bench.

Startled, Susan turned to her maid. "Yes, certainly, Rose. I only want to spend a few moments with my mother and then we will leave." She appreciated that Rose always gave her privacy when she visited her mother's grave, while fully realizing her maid gave it only because she enjoyed a quick nap.

Susan heard the bench squeak behind her as the older woman eased into the small seat. Within minutes, soft snores from her sleeping chaperone rent the air. With the older woman asleep, Susan felt free to talk.

Brushing back a sudden tear, she whispered, for the hundredth time, the monument's inscription to herself. *Visits here do not get any easier.*

ANNA, LADY SATTERFIELD

BELOVED WIFE AND MOTHER

SEPTEMBER 1784 TO DECEMBER 1813

I have so much to tell you, Mama. Moments here were special. The little girl who still dwelled deep inside Susan felt that her mother was still with her, protecting and watching over her.

"It will be dark soon, Mama. I must not stay long. There is a storm coming…" She heard a loud snore and glanced behind her at her maid. *Still she sleeps. The sky could fall, and Rose would sleep through it,* Susan mused. Papa would be angry with her. Little she did annoyed him, but she knew with certainty that she would answer for being out this late without his knowledge. It was her habit to visit her mother's grave every Saturday, but usually, the visits were much earlier in the day.

"I know you would not approve of my coming when dusk is falling, but I needed to speak to you. I have so many things to talk about…" She inhaled a deep breath. "I miss you, Mama." An icy wind blew against her, whipping up her pale yellow wool skirt and slapping it against her legs. She tucked her head down and wrapped herself more tightly in her cloak, pulling it close and buttoning it. The chill slicing the air was frigid. Though Susan shared Rose's fear, she fought against it. Yet the overcast sky, the creaking tree above her and the sudden high-pitched wind whistling through the gravestones added to her already growing sense of eeriness and apprehension. Susan usually coveted the peace she found here, especially since her father's remarriage, but could not displace the anxiety she felt this visit.

"I overheard Papa speaking with Prucilla this morning, Mama. They have made plans for me I know you would not have approved." She poured her heart out to her mother. "I am to marry. It seems he has come to an arrangement with an earl. Goodness! I was so upset, I forgot to ask the name of the lecherous old earl," she whispered aloud, the realization striking her at that moment.

"He is probably an old codger with yellowed, broken, and missing teeth and a weighty paunch hanging over his belt."

She shuddered at the made-up description. "What can I possibly do to prevent such a marriage?" Her voice trembled.

Susan had brought with her a small bouquet of white and yellow roses. She laid the flowers on top of her mother's gravestone and struggled to keep her own tears from watering them. The roses were her mother's favourite. She could close her eyes and envision her mother's face, but time was making it more and more difficult to hear her voice. Susan felt Mama's presence, though—always. It is what kept her coming to the cemetery. Her mother listened.

Mama had been a joyful lady, always laughing and smiling. While always a stickler for polite behaviour and what was proper for *little ladies*, as she often referred to her daughter, she had also encouraged playtime. Her mother had made everything, even learning, fun. Susan had practised all the accomplishments deemed necessary in a young lady, and all the time. Her mother had a list. Ballroom dancing, painting, pianoforte, and gardening—not to mention manners and etiquette which always came at the head of the list. Her mama's enthusiasm was infectious and always encouraging. They would play duets on the pianoforte, paint surprise pictures, and sometimes persuade Papa to dance with her.

Rose had been Mama's loyal companion. Susan still felt a connection to her mother through the maid. If the latter sat still for above ten minutes, Susan could safely predict the older woman would doze, and increasingly, her afternoon naps had become longer. Susan kept this to herself, knowing that if she voiced something, Prucilla, her stepmother, would at once turn Rose off without a reference.

Sleep had come quickly to the abigail this afternoon. Mayhap the shopping trip this morning had been too much for her, and Susan chided herself for having spent so much time looking for silly frippery. Mama had died shortly after Susan's little brother, Alexander, was born. In the beginning,

Susan visited with her father, but the visits were sporadic. She had visited her mother's grave often, always without her father, who seemed to have stopped his visits when he remarried.

Hugging herself, she wiped away another tear, the only outward evidence she would allow of the grief she still felt.

"Mama, if you were still here, things would be different. Papa would not be casting me away." She drew a trembling breath. "I have tried to like Prucilla, but she is unkind, especially to Alex, and I do not trust her."

A small gust of wind swirled around in front of her, catching dead leaves and spinning them into the air. *Take care of your brother. Keep him with you. Have trust in your papa.* The words were clear and resounded throughout her being. Alarmed, she looked around, yet saw no one. She would swear it was her mother's voice, a voice she had thought she would never hear, or be able to recreate in her mind, again— and she had just heard it! She had heard her mother's answer. A startling sense of calm settled over her, and she knew what to do. Her little brother, Alex, had suddenly taken very ill these past two months. He had always been the picture of health. His paleness and lack of strength worried her. He had stopped playing outside and preferred to sit quietly. *He is only six.* Surely... she cut herself off in mid-sentence; she refused to think any bad thoughts. Not here, not now. She would take care of her brother. Maybe a match was the answer. Perhaps her brother could live with her—if Papa would permit it. He must realize that Prucilla did not like Alex.

The bitterly stiff wind whipped up again and blustered, with gusts taking aim at trees and anything in its path. Dust and decayed rose petals swirled; empty branches swayed, dipped, and snapped. The loud crack above her was sudden and gave no warning. The limb came down in a ponderous, lumbering motion, yet allowing her no chance for escape.

Before she could move, it crushed her to the ground under a heavy cover of withered branches. Although she screamed, she did not hear her own voice. Icy fear filled her, her ears only hearing a loud rushing sound.

The storm appeared out of nowhere and moved quickly, so Lord Grayson Harding—Earl Harding, now—decided to take a well-known short-cut across the rear of the Winslow property, which lay adjacent to Bellmane, his family residence. It was the first time he had returned home since his brother's funeral.

He was almost across the Winslow estate when he noticed a carriage parked at the family's graveyard. He reined in his horse, concerned that something had happened, but realized quickly that a family member was paying their respects. The sight of the Marquess of Satterfield's family crest on the carriage sparked a strange sensation inside him. He drew his gelding, Blacklock, to a standstill to see. He had not yet seen his friend, Lady Susan Winslow. If truth be told, it had been several years, but he hoped for a glimpse. *She has been in my thoughts much of late. I hope I may speak to her before the Marquess does.* Thinking of her gave him reason to smile. He had met with her father only two days ago, but had not seen his friend.

It was almost evening, and he felt sure she would not be out here at such an hour, but as he approached, he saw that the petite figure was indeed Lady Susan. His heart filled with the familiar sense of home he always experienced when he thought of her.

Slowing to wave, he called out, but at that moment an enormous rush of wind blew. His horse, a high-couraged steed, reared on his hind legs in panic. A loud crack followed.

CHAPTER 2

Grayson's heart leaped into his throat, rendering him speechless, and he watched, helpless, as the wind dashed an enormous branch on top of his friend where she knelt over a grave. He leaped off his horse and ran to help, followed by two menservants. The huge, bushy limb was lying directly over her head and he feared for the worst. Frantically, he threw off the small limbs and tried to move the large one.

"Men, over here. Give me a hand." The three of them took hold of the giant tree limb. It could have been mistaken for a full-sized tree itself, its girth was so great. Grunting with effort, they heaved the limb up and moved it away from the inert form as quickly as they could.

"My lord, can you tell, is she breathing? She is bleeding!" Lady Susan's companion began fussing to remove the debris from her charge's face, crying and praying with each effort.

Grayson grabbed the girl's hand, assuring himself that she was not mortally wounded. Her pulse pounded. He moved her hair from her face, and beyond a small, bloody gash on the forehead, she seemed unharmed. Yet he could not be sure until she awoke. Gently, he shook her shoulders and spoke to her, trying to rouse her.

"Susan, can you open your eyes?" He leaned closer to her face. Her breaths were strong. She blinked, and then opened her amber eyes, causing his heart to hitch. Grayson remembered how they had been wont to sparkle; they had always reminded him of the glint of sunlight on a pond. Although Susan seemed well enough, he still could not be certain. Besides the gash, she appeared somewhat dazed.

F eeling numb, she opened her eyes, at first to darkness and then to gradual light as the weatherworn branches were lifted from over her. Strong, warm hands pushed her blonde curls back away from her face, and she gazed into the green eyes of a long-ago friend. His welcoming smile calmed her, and the loud singing in her ears ebbed.

Slowly, she could hear sounds and voices again—primarily Rose's, who was screaming words she could only barely make out. "M'lady... oh, gracious heavens! M'lady... it was the crow! He warned us, he did. It was bad luck. I told you."

She heard panicked male voices and felt the pressure of the branches moving. Then there was more frantic crying. Rose. Although she could not distinguish what the maid was saying, Susan tried to move an arm, anything to let the woman know she was all right.

Rose frantically brushed at the grime and twigs covering Susan's yellow wool gown.

"My lady. Susan. Are you harmed?" A warm, masculine voice, full of concern, spoke to her—its husky tones soothing her nerves with each syllable. His large, warm hand brushed away a dead leaf which still lay on her forehead. She gazed at him, comforted by his familiar face—one she had not seen in years. He looked back at her from those worried green eyes, framed by slightly long, curly dark brown hair. She recognized that handsome face with the adorable, dimpled chin. She tried to raise her head, attempting to grip the overgrown grass beneath her for support.

"You are hurt." He took out his handkerchief and wiped blood away from her forehead.

Mechanically, her hand went to her head, and she felt a rather large wet gash above her right eye. Blinking hard, she squinted at her rescuer. "What happened?" She lifted her hand to her temple. "I have the headache a little."

"There has been an accident, my lady."

"Gr… Gr… Grayson?" Not trusting this new reality, she closed her eyes and opened them again. *It is Grayson.* How long had it been since she had seen his smile? The boy she had grown up with was now the most handsome gentleman she had seen—*ever.*

The last time she had seen Grayson Harding, he was waving at her from the crossroads where the small road that joined their properties met the main road. She recalled the dull pain in her chest and the hot tears which had streamed down her face. At twelve years old, she had just waved goodbye to her best friend and was afraid they would never see each other again. She had watched her childhood friend brush back tears as he waved *goodbye*, recognizing that he was as frightened of leaving home as she was of losing her friend. Then her mama had told her he could be gone for several years and had encouraged her to spend more time with her cousins and other friends. That had been a bitter blow to her dwindling hopes. The Harding estate, Bellmane, bordered her father's, and the households had been friendly and close in those early years while both families were growing up. However, that was long ago. With a few exceptions, she had not heard from his family for a considerable time.

Three years ago, Papa had told her that Grayson had moved on to the University to study medicine. More recently, she had learned of Grayson's older brother, Elliot, dying from the Influenza, his title passing to Grayson. She had been saddened by the news of Elliot's death, but they had not been good friends since he had been three years older than Grayson. It had been the friendship of the ladies which had kept the families close. When Mama had died, the two families had gradually lost contact.

"How is it you are here, Grayson, or should I say Lord Harding, now?" She could not stop staring at his face. It was unseemly, particularly since she was practically affianced. *Practically... but not yet.* A smile crept to her lips.

"I confess I was on my way home and took our old short-cut to outrun the storm… which brings to mind a good question. What are *you* doing here at this hour?" He discreetly glanced at Rose—now wide-awake—and whispered, "You bring a sleeping chaperone?"

Susan turned her head, unsure of how to answer. How much had he seen of Rose? When had he arrived?

"Whatever do you mean, 'sleeping'? She is awake," she retorted in a low whisper, struggling to regain her composure. *How dare he question her when he had not bothered even to write to her before today?* When Grayson first left for school, she wrote to him often, keeping him apprised on her animals and adventures, about everything she was doing.

Almost a year went by and there was never a word or responding letter from him, so after a while she stopped writing. Having been confronted by her governess, who delivered a stern reprimand on the etiquette of writing letters and told Susan severely that proper young ladies did not write to young gentlemen, Susan thought it easier to comply. While she did not understand how such dictates could apply to a twelve-year-old child, she knew better than to question the woman and incur her wrath. Still, it was strange how her governess had learned of the clandestine missives, since the only person who had known about them had been Rose. Rose had offered to frank the letters for her, and Susan had never questioned that. To adapt to her new teacher, she had dismissed it all as part of her governess' sour nature.

Her words of a headache added to his concern. From his short time in practice as a doctor, before losing his father and then his elder brother, he knew it could be something more serious.

"Lady Susan Winslow." He tried to ignore the frantic older woman, who was wringing her hands and wailing about a crow and bad luck. "How do you feel? That was quite a blow you took."

"Grayson, I cannot believe you are here." Her eyes searched his.

"Yes, it is I, in the flesh." He flashed a warm smile, relieved that she recognized him. "Wait." He dabbed her forehead with his handkerchief again. "'Tis but a small gash. Head wounds bleed profusely. You will see when the blood is cleaned away. You could have a goose egg by morning. It is swelling already."

Susan tried to get up, but he urged her back. "How is it you are here?"

"Allow me." Getting to his feet, he bent down and picked her up.

"M'lady, are you all right? I was so afraid..." Her maid

rushed forward and hugged Susan, still fussing and picking off leaves which had attached themselves to her dress.

"The pain is tolerable, Rose. I do have a stupid headache now."

"You must go home at once, Lady Susan." He nodded towards the carriage.

Susan turned to the groom and footman. "Isaac, Daniel, thank you both." Clearly concerned, they both seemed to exhale at once, nodded in acknowledgement, and returned to the carriage. The footman opened the doors and pulled a grey wool blanket from under the seat.

Grayson could not stop himself from thinking of her as just Susan. Supporting her slight body against his chest, he walked gingerly, so as not to give her more of a headache. He could smell the jasmine in her hair and fought the urge to bury his head in it. He had never forgotten that she always smelled of jasmine. Impulsively, he bent his head and dropped a small, chaste kiss on the top of her head. Realizing the impropriety of his impulsiveness, he looked up to make sure they had not seen him. Her maid trailed behind him, while the groom and footman were both engaged in readying the carriage. *I would not want her to think badly of me. I must be more careful.*

On reaching the carriage, he helped her inside and covered her with the blanket the footman handed to him. "If it pleases you, ladies, I would like to ride along with you—inside the carriage. Allow me a minute, please, so I might secure Blacklock to the back."

"Certainly, my lord." Rose nodded.

"Yes, Grayson... Lord Harding, I mean." Susan corrected herself.

"I am still Grayson to you... Lady Susan. We are childhood friends, after all."

She reached over and squeezed his hand, sending an odd jolt to his heart. "Susan. Please call me Susan."

Grayson tied Blacklock to the back of the carriage and then settled himself across from the two women.

The carriage started off with a heave, but steadied quickly. Grayson noticed Susan wince.

"How bad is the headache, Susan?" Concerned, he leaned over her and pushed back the blonde curls which were falling in disarray around her face.

"Most of the pain seems to be in the back of my head, but my eyes are rather sore. Mayhap it is the light."

She swayed slightly, and his concern soared. His medical knowledge fed his concern. "Stay awake now, my lady. You will wish to explain all of this to your father. Besides, how would it appear if we arrived, and you were asleep?"

A drowsy giggle greeted this sally. His brow creasing, he admonished her lightly as the vehicle rattled along the stone drive.

"I was delighted, if surprised, to see you out so late and at such a remote location. You are aware, of course, there is a storm on its way?"

"We 'ad been shopping, m'lord, and m'lady wished to see her mother…I mean her mother's grave… before proceedin' 'ome." Rose pointed to a small stack of hatboxes and purchases in the corner beside her, partially hidden by a rolled up, worn brown mantle.

Since his own father had died, Grayson's mother had begun putting an inordinate pressure on him to marry—a pressure she had increased when Elliot died. Mama routinely gave small tea parties with her friends and invited their débutante daughters. He was required to attend briefly and for months now had worked hard to find every reason not to be there. If she trapped him into attending, he found a reason to dash away. He was not proud of his actions, but his mother's behaviour was most inconvenient, and it made him dread seeing her. He had received no communications or messages from Susan and still felt a mixture of hurt and confusion that she had not responded as promised when he went to school, despite his having written to her.

Gradually, he had written letters and tied them in a ribbon, deciding to give them to her when he saw her next. Then, finally, he had stopped writing altogether. It had been a long time—*over six years*—since he had seen her, but he had never forgotten his best friend. There had been other friends and ladies, but no one to take her place in his heart.

She is far more beautiful than I even imagined. I would very much like to take her for a ride and see if she is still the Susan I have always known. Perhaps she would be amenable to a visit tomorrow.

"Susan, do you often visit the cemetery so late in an evening?" he repeated, realizing his irritated tone too late when she wordlessly raised her brows in his direction. *Still the spitfire, I see.* Softening his tone, he continued, "That sounded harsh. I apologize." After a pause, he added, "I am only concerned for your safety."

"You are still overbearing, my lord. After all these years of nary a word from you, you... presume... to chastise me?" Indignation dripped from each word.

He was so taken aback by her fit of temper, he almost missed what she had said to him. "Wait... what did you say?"

"You left here on that day, long ago, and you did not reply to a single letter. I never saw you again. Then, without warning, you reappear today..." She suddenly stopped speaking and stared at his face. "What is it? Why are you smiling at me like that, Grayson?"

"You said you had received no word from *me*?" He grinned. "No letters reached me from you, either." He noted Susan's look of confusion. This conversation had come about a deal quicker than he had planned. "I don't understand. I wrote to you at least every week and gave the notes to my headmaster to frank, with money to cover the post. He had told me it would go out with the other students' mail."

"And I gave mine to... Rose." They both turned and looked at the older woman sitting next to him. Her cheeks flamed as she looked away.

"M'lord, I am undone. Lady Susan, I did it for the best. You were so 'eartbroken when the young lord left, I thought to let you write it out and I would just pretend to post. I thought it 'armless enough. Mercy on me, if your mother had caught me posting her daughter's letters to a young man... Humph!" 'Tis not done. I would have lost my position. I should 'ave said something to your mama, but I felt so sad for you and since I had already told you yes, even knowing I should not..." She broke off and dabbed at her eyes with a corner of her shawl. "I am very sorry, my lady, truly I am."

She appeared to be answering honestly, Grayson observed, suppressing a wave of irritation.

"Did you speak with my governess?" Susan demanded.

"Yes," Rose replied, hanging her head. "You wrote lots of letters, and I was afraid your mother would catch me with them." She took a deep breath. "I thought I was doing the right thing."

Susan reached over and squeezed her maid's hand. "It makes sense now." She tittered. "My governess lectured me on propriety and kept introducing the subject of letters and young men. While I thought it odd, I had not considered you might have spoken to her." Turning to Grayson, she continued, "You remember the woman, do you not, sir? I was hiding from her cruelty on the day I accidentally fell from the apple tree near the pond. You remember *that*."

"It is hard to forget sitting under an apple tree and having someone fall in your lap." They both dissolved into laughter.

"I lost my footing and, as I recall, you were the softer option."

Grayson cleared his throat. "Well, we rubbed along pretty well together, Susan. It was always grand sport." He turned back to the maid. "Rose, thank you for looking out for my friend. At least that answers half of the puzzle. As a boy, it would have seemed ridiculous that propriety could prevent two childhood friends from continuing their friendship. Now, as a man, I understand a little better, although there are many rules in Society which seem arbitrary to me."

He studied his fingernails for a moment. "There is still a mystery to be solved, because my letters to Susan from school were not received. I am curious, so I will ask. It is too late to discuss it with my father, whom I thought the only one involved with my schooling, but Mama will surely answer and tell me anything she knows." He sounded surer than he felt. The closeness between the families had ended with Lady Satterfield's death. He had always wondered about that, but on the various occasions he had broached the topic, both of his parents had changed the course of the conversation. He had not been too young to take notice of the tactic, but had soon felt it was useless to pursue his queries.

"We just passed that infamous apple tree." He chuckled. "Your house is around the next bend, if I recall correctly. How is the headache?" He leaned towards Susan in concern.

"It has eased a little, but I still have it." She drew her wrap closer about her. "The wind is rather chilling."

The sound of crunching oyster shells beneath the wheels alerted him they had turned up the drive to the main house.

"The walnut tree we planted near the drive has grown," he observed aloud.

"Ha! Yes. The gardener complained to Papa that we had ruined his landscape, but Papa made sure he allowed it to grow without interference. It makes me think of our escapades when I see it."

He wondered if Lord Satterfield had let Susan know about his visit two days ago. She had not mentioned it, so he presumed not.

To his surprise, Susan's face had turned to abject misery upon entering the drive, as if she were going to her execution. She chewed her bottom lip, an outward sign of what he knew to be her anxiety, and her face paled.

To compound matters, the storm that had threatened earlier suddenly broke free, with driving rain beginning noisily to pelt the carriage. A gust of wind hit the carriage, causing it to tilt alarmingly. Grayson reached over and, resting one hand on each woman's shoulder, steadied them on the seat.

"My apologies, ladies. I meant only to steady you and prevent harm to either of you."

"Thank you, Grayson." Susan wriggled to right herself in the seat. "We are almost home."

"Oh m'lord. 'Tis more of the crow, I fear." Rose crossed herself and muttered a prayer. "'Tis not good at all, not at all m'lady."

Within a few minutes, the rain stopped as abruptly as it started, and the wind calmed again.

"Well, now, how fortuitous… and strange." He peered out of the window, taking in a still stormy view, and wondered when the rain would begin again. He hoped for the best, knowing his own house was near. "Let us not waste good fortune. We are almost to the front door, and the rain has provided respite without adding misery." He would have welcomed more time with Susan and could not help feeling slightly irritated the journey was so short. "Susan, if you are well enough soon, I would very much like to take you for a carriage ride—or mayhap a picnic—depending on how you are feeling, of course." He hoped to cheer her with the suggestion.

"Grayson... I should like that very much."

"Marvellous." A grin spread across his face he could not depress. "Yes, indeed, sir. How pleasant it will be. I will be excited to go, and Rose may bring a pot of Cook's plum jam."

Ah, yes, her sleepy chaperone would, of course, be joining them. *Perfect. I want to find out more of what is happening in that house, and I need someone to be on my side.* Following on the thought, he remembered Susan had accused him of being overbearing. *I need to take a more cautious route in order to woo my lady.*

CHAPTER 3

*S*usan hated that the carriage ride home was so short with Grayson. She really should have said something to him about her *almost betrothal* when he asked about an outing, but on a whim, she had decided not to. After all, she was not officially betrothed—and she hoped against hope that things could change in her favour. She threw caution to the wind. *I cannot wait to go on an outing with Grayson. There are so many things I want to ask him, so much time to bridge.* Being back in his company felt right; it was as if their friendship had continued through the years, and she hoped he felt the same. She could have sworn he gave her a kiss on the head when he carried her to the coach, but she was too dazed to be certain. Was there any hope that Grayson might care for her?

Maybe she could convince her father not to sign the marriage settlements. She sighed heavily. It was not likely. She had not seen Grayson in years, but that part of her life had never been far from her mind. He had always saved her from one catastrophe or another—it had been how they had met each other. Whether it was getting stuck in a tree after climbing too high, falling out of a tree while hiding from her dragon governess, getting thrown from her horse, stung by a bee, or standing too far back on the edge of a pond and losing her balance, Grayson had always been her hero, there to help. She exhaled. *When you put it all together, I sound like quite the damsel in distress. Now this happens. Grayson has not quite saved my life, but he was there once again to rescue me. He is like a hero from my books.* Her best friend was back and, true to form, he had rescued her from certain death beneath a walnut tree branch. That could be a book title. She snorted out loud, and Rose and Grayson both turned to her.

"Ha! Did you just... *snort?*" Grayson gave a rich, mellow laugh, and his cheery tone was contagious. She smiled, restraining herself from laughing only because her head was throbbing.

As they pulled into the drive leading to her home, a rider tipped his hat as he passed them, travelling in the opposite direction.

"Was that Lord Munster?" she muttered under her breath.

"Why yes, I believe it *was* the Earl of Munster. Perhaps he had business with your father."

What? Surely not the business of betrothal? An icy fear added to the misery and headache she was already feeling. Even she, with her limited access to *ton* events, knew of Lord Munster. He was good looking, but rumour was he could be cruel. *Surely Papa is not considering him?*

"He draws up his bottom lip and upper teeth together, bunny-like, and makes a sucking noise through them after he speaks—a most annoying habit," she complained aloud before she could stay the words. Grayson looked at her, cocking his head in question at her statement. "I am sorry. That was rude. I am ashamed I remarked upon it."

"Why would you even concern yourself with him?" Grayson asked.

"I have only met him once, but it was most memorable. Prucilla and Papa held a dinner party, and Lord Munster was in attendance. I should have been more prudent with my comments, Grayson."

A smile stretched across his face. "Pleasant-looking fellow, but he has that annoying habit." He leaned close. "I should not encourage you in such outbursts..." He chuckled. "... but I stand back when speaking to him, myself. The habit can be distracting."

Yes, and marriage to him would be horrible. Prucilla would like such a husband for her, Susan was certain. She held her head, trying to temper the pain, which had just increased.

The carriage pulled to a stop before a three-storied, golden ashlar stone mansion, built in the Palladian style and topped by four large classical statues. The lowest floor's stone facade was rough-faced, while the top two floors were flat and even. Four columns framed a Corinthian portico that dominated the front. Directly over its massive grey wooden door hung stone laurels and medallions, which drew attention to the second floor, reached only by two branching flights of stone steps. Daniel opened the door to the carriage and set out a small iron step for her to alight.

She had bigger problems at the moment than the height of the vehicle. They were almost at her door and Grayson would be off to his own home.

"Lady Susan, while I am here, I should like to have a word with your father."

"Certainly, Lord Harding." Unsure of the root of her irritation, she answered tersely, deciding to use his titled name.

He raised his brows. "There is something I would like to discuss with him. It will not take long."

The door opened, and an aged man stepped forward. Gibbs, her family's long-time butler, started at seeing her bedraggled appearance.

"Lady Susan, your father has been beside himself with worry. Forgive me, my lady…" He leaned closer and peered at her forehead. "Are you well? What has happened?"

She did not have a chance to answer.

"Daughter, where have you been?" Her father's harried voice came from behind Gibbs. "Prucilla and I have suffered severe agitation of the spirits worrying for your well-being. Did you not notice the change in the weather and the time?"

Susan winced at the sound of her papa's voice. Wearing a queer smile on her lips, her stepmother followed her father; Susan's head throbbed madly. The woman was not her mother, and she grew tired of the pretence. She doubted very much that her stepmother ever worried about her.

"Father, I assure you I am quite well." Susan looked behind her and then felt Grayson's hand at her elbow. Warmth at once radiated up her arm.

"Lord Harding! This is an unlooked-for surprise. How is it you are with my daughter?" Her father halted abruptly when Grayson stepped forward.

Close on his heel, Prucilla bumped into her husband's back when he stopped, banging her face against his shoulder.

"I would appreciate it if you would warn me, husband, if you intend to stop suddenly," she snapped, rubbing her nose.

"Prucilla… wife, you should keep a proper distance." The Marquess turned around and gave his wife a frosty stare. "I should like some time alone with my daughter." He fixed her with what Susan always described as 'the look'. It was when Papa narrowed his eyes and quirked an eyebrow—a deeply condescending look he usually reserved for occasions of great import. She had seen it often enough to recognize it well.

Susan bit her lip to keep from laughing, but wondered why Papa was so put out with Prucilla. She had heard them arguing, but it seemed they were of accord with the betrothal. She suddenly recalled her father accusing Prucilla of not having her best interests in mind, and tried to think what that could mean. But it only added to her megrim. There had to be something else, something she had not recognized as important. As she considered this, she could not prevent a small sliver of hope from growing in her chest.

"Daughter, your forehead is bleeding. Come into the drawing room." He directed Susan across the entrance hall and into the large room decorated in shades of blue and white. She sat down on a blue floral sofa while her father turned to Rose. "Send the groom for the doctor."

"Papa, I am sorry I caused you distress." She felt contrite and tried to speak, despite the pain in her head. "After shopping, I stopped at the cemetery to speak with Mother. So much happened this morning. I needed time to reflect. A storm blew up and the branch of a tree fell on me, but I am not badly hurt." To give her hands something to do, she brushed at her dress, picking off a leaf which had escaped Rose's notice.

"'Tis true, my lord. Whilst I was sitting there, giving my lady a bit of time with her dearly departed mother. I barely closed…" Rose coughed nervously. "… I mean, settled myself comfortably, and the largest tree limb I ever saw came crashing down."

"It is true, Papa. The wind came up and the next thing I knew, Daniel and Lord Harding were pulling the branch away from me."

"What?" His face went ashen.

She could not be sure she had ever seen her even-tempered Papa so frightened. His expression was one of complete shock.

My wretched tongue. She realized her response had been too glib. "Papa, I am so… sorry. Forgive me. I did not mean that to sound so simplistic. The storm moved quickly; I was frightened to death. However, fortune then favoured me, for Grayson... Lord Harding arrived."

"Lord Satterfield, although I no longer practice medicine since accepting my title, I am still a qualified doctor. I examined Susan's wound and I think she may have a slight concussion, but hopefully nothing too serious. She has a headache and a nasty swelling. To be on the safe side, though, perhaps she should remain awake and sit quietly for the next few hours. That is the current thinking with injuries to the head."

"Thank you, Lord Harding. My wife and I appreciate your help, and we are thankful you were there to assist our daughter." Seating himself beside her, Papa lifted Susan's chin and studied her face, almost ensuring himself of her good health.

"Ahem." Grayson cleared his throat politely. "May I have a moment of your time, my lord? Perhaps in your library?"

"Oh. Yes...certainly, Lord Harding." Her father struggled to hide his surprise, but made a quick recovery. "It is good to see you back in these parts again." He arched his eyebrows as he spoke. "Daughter, you seem to be recovering, but I would feel better if you would allow Lord Harding..." He cleared his throat awkwardly. "... to conduct a proper examination. Lord Harding, if you would consent. Rose dispatched the groom for Dr. Steth, but it may be hours before he can be here, should he be with other patients. It would relieve my mind."

Susan looked past her father to Grayson, whose own face remained neutral of expression. *I would love to have him examine me.*

"Yes, Papa, if it would please you."

"Good. I believe it would ease my mind. Lord Harding, would you object? We can step into the library when you have completed your examination." Her father stepped aside, and moving forward, Grayson kneeled down by her side.

"Certainly, Lord Satterfield." Grayson nodded. He looked pleased at this turn of events. He captured Susan's gaze; his concern was apparent. "My lady, how are you feeling?"

"A little better, my lord. My head does not feel as it should, but I have had these megrims before."

"With your permission, I would like to try something that could give me a considerable measure of comfort as to your condition." The warmth in his expression invited trust.

She nodded.

"I need..." He looked around the room and pointed to the candle on her mother's escritoire, which stood nearby. "May I use that?"

Her father concurred and handed it to him. "Susan, I would like you to follow the light with your eyes without moving your head."

Certainly, Grayson. I would follow you anywhere. "Yes. I think I can do that." She carefully tracked the candle, trying hard not to focus instead on his green eyes, which seemed to twinkle in the taper's glow.

He moved the candle back and forth. "I am very relieved to see that you can follow the light without moving your head. Lord Satterfield, would you send for some alcohol and soft, clean cloths? I would like to clean this nasty cut. It does not, fortunately, appear to need a stitch."

"Certainly." The Marquess pulled the bell, and the footman appeared. "Daniel, will you fetch some alcohol from my library?"

"Yes, my lord."

Daniel returned quickly. "Lord Harding, I have the alcohol and cloths."

"Thank you, Daniel." Grayson turned to Susan. "This will sting a little." He poured alcohol on the clean cloth and applied it to her wound, gently.

"Ouch!" Susan groaned. "It stings."

"Yes, I apologize for that. But I needed to make sure the wound was clean of debris." Grayson placed the alcohol and the dirty rag on the floor near them. He took another dry cloth and dabbed the area around the cut, drying it and soothing the ache the alcohol had brought.

The touch of Grayson's hand to Susan's head sent a delicious warm tremor down her neck and Susan leaned forward, almost in a trance. She was enjoying this far too much.

He eased her head from side to side. "Does this hurt?"

"No, the movement itself does not trouble me, but it adds to my headache a little."

"That is a good sign," he uttered softly.

Grayson finished the examination and turned to her father. "Lord Satterfield, Susan seems to have escaped serious affliction, except for the headache and this abrasion. Perhaps a little laudanum from the doctor, if you do not have some to hand, would be in order should she feel out of sorts and in pain. I encourage limiting usage of the drug, though. It is my contention that the more awareness she maintains, the better to gauge the extent of her injury. Sleep would not allow us to know if a further problem presents itself. Concussions are a subject of great concern and have received much more attention since Waterloo." He walked back to her mother's desk and returned the candle.

It is over? Susan wanted a longer examination but knew better than to utter a word. She wanted more of that feeling, which seemed to come the moment he touched her.

"Susan, please remain in here. I wish to speak with you on my return." Her father's voice interrupted her thoughts. She nodded, and the two men left the drawing room together.

She could not imagine why her father would speak to Grayson in his library in such a nonsensical fashion. Grayson had initiated it. It was quite extraordinary. Why would her old friend wish to be closeted with Papa? No doubt it was because of her headache, but the whole situation was too smoky by half, as her groom was wont to remark.

Her father had always been good to her... until he had married Prucilla. Somehow, Susan had resisted laughing out loud at the look on Prucilla's face when Papa had dismissed her. His wicked, rebellious daughter wished he might do that again... and again. It had given her great joy to see it, and although she ought to feel guilt for such an admission, she could not find it in her to do so. Never would Papa have spoken so scornfully to Mother, and that thought made her smile all the more. Evidently matters were not nearly as sunny as Prucilla liked to portray. Her stepmother sapped happiness from a room the minute she appeared, and her father rarely seemed happy nowadays.

Shaking herself from her disgraceful thoughts, she turned her gaze to her maid, standing patiently with her hands clasped.

"Rose, I feel sure that Grayson will ask Papa's permission to take me for the ride he mentioned." *Please, Papa, do not spoil this outing. I dearly wish to have someone special to think about before I have to marry the Earl you have promised me to.* "I told you what I heard this morning. Unless I can convince Father to give me a chance to be presented to Society, I shall be married off to someone I am sure Prucilla has picked."

"I fear you are correct, m'lady. Since your father married again, a terrible tension has come over this house. I should not say this, but I do not think she likes your brother, and for the life of me..." Her maid stopped talking when the sound of footsteps approached the door. She lowered her voice to a whisper. "We will do our best."

"Rose, will you please see how Alex does?" she asked, remembering the ethereal words of her mother. *Take care of your brother.*

"Yes, m'lady, at once."

"If he is not sleeping, ask him to join me. I would like to introduce him to Grayson... Lord Harding."

"Yes, m'lady." The older woman left the room and could be heard tramping heavily up the stairs.

Determined to make the best of it, Susan considered the promise she had made to her mother. It was more of a mental promise than one expressed to that lady. If she married, it was inevitable she would lose the chance to have a Season. Married ladies could not be brought out; they were out! Her father had decided, and Prucilla would ensure she married the old toad.

While Prucilla protested a friendship with her mother, Susan very much doubted Mother would have been this woman's friend. They were not remotely alike. Prucilla continually inserted herself into the family, pulling the wool over Papa's eyes with her feigned willingness to care for Alex, while spurning the necessity for Susan to have a Season. *She is deliberately undermining my opportunity to enjoy a Season. Yet, how can I when Alex is so very sick and no one quite knows what is wrong?*

"Oh, Mama, I wish you were here," she whispered towards the heavens. "We all miss you."

The slight movement caused a twinge of pain. Reaching up, she felt the growing knot on her forehead and smiled. Yes, it hurt, but not sorely enough to wish it away. After all, she was sure Grayson was here because of it.

CHAPTER 4

$\mathcal{G}$rayson followed Lord Satterfield to his office, wondering what Susan knew or did not know. He had met with the Marquess last week at his club. Susan seemed surprised to see him, and when he asked her for an excursion, he had the distinct feeling that she did not know of the betrothal in progress. "Come in, Lord Harding. Have a seat." Satterfield pointed to the two mahogany elbow chairs in front of his matching mahogany desk. Grayson chose the one on the left and a small black cat came out of nowhere and jumped into the one on the right, purring loudly.

"Who?" Grayson leaned over and petted the feline. Satterfield chuckled. "You mean, whose cat? That is Noelle—she is Susan's and has the run of the house. She appeared on the porch one day and ran through Gibbs' legs, straight to Susan —just before Anna, Susan's mother, died. Susan swore she had never seen her before, but the cat certainly seemed to know her. Prucilla is not fond of cats—she claims they make her sneeze, but the cat is a good mouser, and stays out of the way. This is her home as long as Susan lives here."

"Meaning?" He chuckled to himself. This was the first he had heard of a cat, not that it changed anything. Grayson had neither lived in proximity to cats nor ever considered owning one. Rather in the way of farm animals, they were just *there*... hanging about the kitchens and the stable yard. Dismissing the cat, he considered the Marquess, eager to get to his point.

"Lord Satterfield, I am not concerned about the cat, I assure you. There is, however, a different matter I wish to discuss with you."

"I think I know what is on your mind. If you are wondering when I will tell her, I have yet to..."

Grayson cut him off. "Begging your pardon, Lord Satter-field, but I wish to woo your daughter before you inform her."

"*Woo her?*" He sounded incredulous. "Do you mean to say you wish to take her on excursions—go for strolls in the parkland and suchlike?"

"Well, yes, I believe I do..." Grayson replied cautiously, unsure why the idea was so foreign to Susan's father. He had heard it said that her parents had experienced a love-match. "It is my wish, if possible, to create a good beginning for the match. I was reminded today that Susan is given to resisting circumstances forced upon her, and I do not wish to be seen as 'dictatorial.'"

Satterfield brightened. "Ah, yes, woo her by all means at your disposal, sir!" He beamed. "May I pour you a drink, Lord...?"

"Harding... please to call me Harding, my lord. You will be my father-in-law soon, and I would prefer it."

"Thank you, Harding. He unlocked a small cupboard and pulled out a decanter of cognac and two glasses. "Here, my boy." He poured a small quantity into each glass and handed one to Harding. "This is from the last barrel bought by my father before the hostilities. Perhaps I should tell you what she knows."

"Yes. That might be important. Let us start there." Grayson took a swallow and set his glass in front of him on the desk.

"You know Susan. She has not changed—she still marches to the beat of her own drummer. Sometimes she misses the beat, but she will defy you to tell her." Her father guffawed as he evidently recollected their earlier conversation. "I suspect Susan may have overheard Prucilla and I talking about her betrothal. I cannot be sure, of course, but I think she only caught the end of the conversation. Prucilla and I had not agreed, exactly, but that is rather beside the point. She marched in here as soon as Prucilla had left and started arguing with me, begging me to give her at least this Season. I told her I had already arranged a betrothal to an earl, but no more than that. I did not mention a name." He took a big swallow of his drink, placed his glass in front of him, and leaned forward on his arms, hands gripping the sides of the desk. "She does not know the earl is you. I would wager she believes I have tied her to an ageing reprobate with little hair."

Grayson nearly choked on his drink, spewing it over the front of his coat. "She would not think that of you."

"Oh, but she would believe it of my wife. Prucilla and my daughter do not see eye to eye. Although there is an air of friction between them, I assure you, Susan has been nothing other than polite. I am not sure why I am telling you this. Perhaps it is because you will soon be a part of the family." He took a deep breath before continuing. "She is my daughter, and I know her well. I am aware she is both hurt and angry with me for directing her life in this."

His expression turned serious, and he fortified himself with another gulp from his glass.

"I have not seen you in a long time, Harding. Nonetheless, I know you to be an honest and caring young man. It is my belief you will deal well with Susan, and you have a friendship on which to build a good marriage." He let out a tremulous breath. "I should apologize for my sentiment. Her mother, rest her soul, would approve of you."

"Thank you, Lord Satterfield. There is no need for an apology. On that last note, I should like to escort Susan on a carriage ride this week, depending on how she feels. I thought we might drive to Edward Park or take in the Pavilion."

Satterfield nodded his approval, fumbling through a pile of papers on the corner of his desk.

"Ah. Here it is." Smiling, he waved the missive at Grayson. "I trust you will also have one of these. It is bound to be the biggest party of the Season. I had planned to take Susan and Prucilla, but after speaking with you earlier this week, I changed my mind, as her future seemed secured. On reflection, I think it would be the very thing for a spot of wooing." He chuckled. "It is a Christmastide celebration and takes place in two weeks."

Opening the centre drawer to his desk, he extracted some papers, scratching his head. "I told Susan I planned to sign the betrothal settlements later in the week." He placed the documents in front of them. "I recently received copies from my man of business. Susan will surely expect to know the name of her betrothed by then," he remarked with a laugh. "I still cannot believe she did not ask. I would have told her. Now, however, I find I am going to do everything I can to keep the gentleman's identity from her. It should give you time… to court. Oh! This should be diverting." He rubbed his hands together gleefully.

"Thank you, sir." Grayson had reason to smile. "The party sounds as if it will give me the perfect opportunity. I will look out the invitation when I arrive home. I cannot do aught but approve a plan which allows me more time to win my lady's hand!"

Satterfield stood up and walked over to Grayson, who also rose. Satterfield clapped him on the back.

"Good luck, my boy. Let me know if you need any advice." He sniggered at his own words, causing Grayson to laugh, too.

"Ha. Of course. Thank you, sir." Grayson grinned from ear to ear. Noelle, apparently tired of this male camaraderie, stood and stretched, and then headed towards the door, where she waited, swishing her tail.

"If I did not know better, I would say that cat was spying." Satterfield shook his head and chuckled at his own assertion.

"For Susan? Indeed! She always had a way with animals… not bees, but animals seemed to adore her."

"Yes. I remember the time she became acquainted with the bee population." He slapped his knee in glee. "Go on with you, young man—and good luck. I suppose we should return to Susan. Are you certain she will suffer no further problems?"

"With head injuries, it is hard to tell. She seems to have a good sense of her surroundings, and while she has a headache, it does not seem severe."

They both walked in silence towards the drawing room.

That went well, Grayson thought. As he neared the front door, he saw the maid, Rose, leading a blond, curly-headed boy into the drawing room.

"Alex, sit here beside me." Susan patted the seat next to her.

"What happened, Sue-Sue?" Her brother's small fingers touched the large lump forming above her eye. His voice was slow and quiet. "It is a big bump."

"It is nothing that will not heal." She patted the sofa again.

"I do not want you to worry. Come, sit with me," she repeated. The young man complied and moved to nestle under Susan's right arm.

"Alex, this is my friend, Lord Harding."

"Good evening, young man." Grayson offered his hand.

"Good evening, my lord." Grayson noticed the child's pallor straight away. His skin was so translucent, he could see the blue blood vessels beneath, and his brown eyes were dull. The contrast with Lady Susan's picture of health was startling. Grayson tried not to stare, but the sallowness was remarkable.

"Young man, your sister and I grew up together here-abouts. She was particularly adept at finding trouble." He gave the lad a mischievous smile. "I'll wager she has told you some of her very best adventures."

"No, my lord. We used to run and play outside, but while I am ill, I am not allowed to go out and play. Mostly, I play with my soldiers, or Susan reads to me." Narrowing his eyes, Alex looked at Grayson more closely. "Are you a duke? I want to meet a duke someday."

"No. I am not a duke, but I am an earl. Will that do? In fact, I am just now learning my duties, and maybe you can help me." The little boy smiled and nodded. Not sure why the lad wanted to know someone with a title, Grayson ventured cautiously, "Do you ride, Alex? I have a pony coming to live on my estate this week. He used to belong to friends of my mother, who have removed to London and have decided that they want to find him a suitable home in the country. He lives in London and my groom is bringing him to my estate, which is very close. I believe he would love to have a little boy to ride him, and it would help me because one of my duties is to get to know my land and the people on it. I would enjoy the company."

He noticed Alex's eyes light up. "I have not yet learned to

ride, my lord, but Papa talked to me about getting a horse." He turned and looked beseechingly at his father, waiting for an answer.

The Marquess nodded his approval. "Alex, Lord Harding is most kind to invite you. I would like you to learn to sit a horse. Certainly, it would be good for you to get some fresh air. As long as he rides with you, I see no harm. Be sure and listen to Lord Harding, son."

"Lord Satterfield, you are welcome to accompany him. We can ride over the estate—I would very much appreciate your opinions, since I am new to land ownership."

"My dear, I fear I must protest." The Marchioness entered the room, her words delivered in a whining tone. She looked over at Susan with barely veiled contempt. "Our little lord cannot go outside. He is still afflicted with the stomach complaint. He must stay indoors."

"Prucilla, I have promoted this excursion," her husband answered shortly. "Alex has stayed indoors these two months, and he seems no better. His lordship's pony may be all that Alex needs to bring him back to health. He has been ill since the end of the summer, and I cannot fathom the cause. Sunshine and ponies are just the ticket for small boys."

Lord Satterfield turned back to Grayson and shook his hand. "Thank you. You have put the first smile on my son's face in over two months. Hopefully, the outing will also put some colour back in his cheeks."

He picked up his son, smiling "Alex, this will be enormous fun. Do you mind if I tag along? I should like to see Bellmane myself. It has been years since I rode about the land. The doctor will be here soon enough, to see your sister, and I will get his opinion on your health as well. Does that sound reasonable, Grayson?"

"Certainly, Lord Satterfield." Grayson turned his attention to Susan. "Lady Susan, if I may be so bold, your colour has returned to your cheeks and you seem more at ease. This pleases me greatly, for I wish to beg a favour of you."

"A favour, my lord?" She looked rather perplexed, so he rushed on.

"It would be my pleasure if you would accompany me to the Royal Pavilion on Tuesday. I understand it is wondrous indeed and I have yet to visit."

"Lord Harding…Grayson, I would like to do that. I feel sure I shall have recovered by then from this afternoon's excitement." She beamed.

Rose returned to the room at that moment, accompanied by Dr. Steth. The Marchioness followed them into the room and stood quietly near the door.

"Dr. Steth. Thank you for coming." The relief in Satterfield's voice was clear. "My daughter has had an accident. The limb of a large tree fell on her. Lord Harding, who is also a trained doctor, has examined her. He believes her to have a slight concussion and has instructed us on how to go on. He also recommends laudanum to be used sparingly, if at all. I admit the shock of seeing her injured scared the wits from my head. I sent for you before I remembered Lord Harding is a qualified doctor, and profusely apologize for dragging you out at this hour. However, since you are here, could you examine my boy? We have been invited to Bellmane, and I want you to be in accordance with our plan."

"I will be happy to do so, my lord. Lord Harding, Lady Prucilla, it is good to see you both again. I am pleased to see your daughter sitting upright. It is the best course, I understand, according to the latest studies I have read in the medical journals for falls and head injuries. Lord Satterfield, it seems that my friend, Lord Harding has given you good instruction. Since I am here, would you mind if I take a quick look at both patients?"

"Lord Harding, I apologize most sincerely for my earlier

oversight." The Marquess' face coloured slightly. "I would not have sent for Dr. Steth had I recalled your training earlier. Since he is here, however…"

"Certainly, Lord Satterfield. I assure you, I take no offence. I want what is best for Susan." Grayson stepped aside and provided room for Steth to approach Susan.

The tall, thin doctor nodded politely and pulled up a stool. Sitting across from his first patient, he said, "Lady Susan, please tell me what happened."

Susan leaned back on the cushions and related the events. "Except for this nagging megrim, I feel much better. It was a shock."

Dr. Steth examined Lady Susan. "The cut and the headache do concern me, Lady Susan, yet there does not seem to be anything amiss with your eyes." He reached into his bag and pulled out a small bottle, which he handed to her maid. "I will leave this laudanum for your mistress. Please let her have some only if she has inordinate trouble sleeping because of the headache." He looked down at his patient and continued, "And I would like to know, my lady, if you have any problems with your vision or anything else over the next day or so. I think you should have no further problems. Concussions are hard to diagnose, so be sure to send for me if you have need."

He then turned his attention to Alex and conducted his own examination.

"Lord Satterfield, the young lord's constitution is about the same. I will repeat what I told your wife."

As the doctor continued, Grayson briefly glanced toward Prucilla and watched her expression change to barely suppressed anger.

"She requested I bleed him. I do not believe in bleeding, and especially not in his…" Dr. Steth hesitated. "… sensitive condition. It is my belief that his blood should be allowed to heal and strengthen the body."

"I concur with you, Dr. Steth. Losses further sicken the body," Grayson interjected.

"Well, now! Fresh air may stimulate the appetite and cast pink into those cheeks, young master." The doctor patted Alex's head with gentle affection. Clearly, he liked Alex. "I will take myself off to my supper if you have no further need of me."

"I will leave as well. I thank you for your hospitality, Lord Satterfield, Lady Satterfield." He inclined his head. "Lady Susan, I look forward to our excursion later this week."

Lord Satterfield rang for a footman. "Daniel, have the groom bring Lord Harding's and Dr. Steth's mounts to the front entrance.

"Yes, my lord. Immediately."

Grayson walked outside with Dr. Steth. When the door closed behind them, he tapped the doctor's shoulder.

"Steth, my good man. I wonder if you might join me at my estate tomorrow. It will give me time to look up a few things. I will pay you for your time. I need your opinion on something." Grayson gave a slight shake to his head. "Wait. What is wrong with me? You are leaving, and it is well into the evening. I will be glad to provide you a room to stay the night at Bellmane. We are close and I am leaving as well."

"Lord Harding, I appreciate the offer, but I do not live far from here and have patients who may need to reach me during the night. However, I will be glad to call on you tomorrow. There is no need to pay. A glass of your excellent brandy is all the payment I need. I would like your considered opinion, as well. I think we are of the same mind on this. I will see you tomorrow."

"Until tomorrow then, and thank you."

Grayson walked to his horse, Blacklock, feeling a mixture of relief and anxiousness. The storm which had caused so much havoc had blown past them as quickly as it had arrived, and he saw no damage near the house. It appeared that the tree in the cemetery had been the only casualty. He appreciated any small mercy. Taking the reins from the groom, he mounted, reflecting on all that had taken place in the last few hours. It had been such a long time since he had seen Susan, and then, suddenly, as he had passed the graveyard, there she was. Certainly, the family had changed; the loss of the first Lady Satterfield was evident, especially with her children.

His mother would be concerned when he told her about this visit. The young lord seemed gravely ill. He wanted to help, but how?

Susan was still the person he remembered—as he had hoped—and it brought a slight smile to his lips. The stepmother—the new Lady Satterfield—he had disliked on sight. He planned to ask his mother what she knew about Prucilla and wished he could recall her name before her marriage. There was something not right about her, especially her interest in Alex. He was astonished at Alex's sickly condition, and that was putting it lightly. He had seen these symptoms before and wanted to consult his books to check his memory against them.

It was timely to have the pony coming to Bellmane. The fresh air could be of considerable help to Susan's brother.

One could not help but notice the strained relationships in the household. It was not his business, of course, but Lord Satterfield's demeanour was very different with the current Lady Satterfield. He noticed the friction Lord Satterfield had referred to earlier, but it was not just between Susan and her stepmother. It was not his nature to insert himself into his peer's business, but this was about Susan. He hoped to make her his Countess, and he wanted to know all he could; something seemed at odds in that household.

He looked back at the house, a brooding monolith against the starlit sky, and reaching the road, nudged his horse into a gallop.

"Let us be away home, Blacklock."

CHAPTER 5

*A*n hour later that same evening, Grayson reached his mother's town house in Brighton, in plenty of time for dinner, since Bellmane was only a few miles north-east of town. Striding into the parlour, he found his mother sitting with a guest. Ambrose, Viscount Blaine, a widower with grown children, was ensconced in a deep armchair by the fire and looked quite at home. It was about time, as far as Grayson was concerned. He liked the man and had been informed by a crony that they had seen together Blaine and his mother about the town. It seemed they frequented the theatre, the Pavilion, promenaded on the Grand Parade and even the local tea shops together. He was not at all surprised the Countess was entertaining.

Blaine was an astute businessman with an affable sense of humour. For a man of three-and-fifty, he was in very good health. He was tall and broad shouldered, and his wavy brown hair was only greying at the temples. The pair rubbed along well.

"We were just about to have a small glass of sherry, my dear. Will you join us?"

Grayson leaned over his mother's chair and gave her a kiss on the cheek.

"I would appreciate a drink, ma'am. It has been a very long day. That could be a perfect ending."

"Lord Harding, what is your pleasure? Your mother prefers a glass of sherry, but I have been meditating on this French brandy all afternoon." Blaine gently swirled a deep amber liquid in its crystal decanter. "May I offer you a glass?"

"Thank you. Please, call me Harding."

"Likewise, dispense with formality."

"My two favourite men are here with me tonight for dinner. I could not be happier. This will be a lovely evening. Cook has prepared all of your favourites, Grayson. Turtle soup, a boiled ham and a lemon cake for dessert."

"Thank you, Mother. I think the last time I had lemon cake was... well..." He shook his head and smiled, finishing, "I cannot recall but I think it was here."

They all laughed. "I am looking forward to dinner." Blaine smiled and held up his glass.

"Mother... Blaine..." Grayson looked at the older man and dipped his head slightly. "I would appreciate your help with a certain matter. First, though, I should like to share some news of my own, so you will understand how all of this has come to be. It has yet to be announced, so please do not spread it abroad, Mother."

"Spread what abroad, my son?"

"Lord Satterfield and I have agreed upon the details, and we should sign the contracts tomorrow. Yes, I think that is workable. I have them and he will be at my house, so it will be a perfect time to conclude the formalities." Grayson felt his cheeks burn slightly when he realized he had been talking aloud, yet more to himself than to his mother and her guest.

"Conclude *what*? Grayson, you are speaking in riddles."

His mother leaned forward in her chair, her curiosity palpable.

"Mother, I know you have been concerned and have felt the need to..." He cleared his throat. "...to help me arrange my future."

"Grayson, that is not fair. I have merely been ensuring *both* our futures..." She wore a sly smile.

"Mother, it is impossible for a mother *not* to interfere in her son's affairs." He gave her a mischievous grin. "You may now relax your matchmaking instincts, for I have news to impart. I hope you will feel it is the best news."

"Do not keep me in suspense, dearest. Pray tell us this momentous news." Behind his mother's smile, he discerned a measure of strain.

"Very well. I plan to marry Lady Susan Winslow."

The room went quiet. Grayson looked at his mother, unsure of her reaction to his cannon shot, until a broad smile lit up her face.

"Oh, my darling boy," she declared, opening her arms wide. "I had hoped you would consider Susan. Anna would be so pleased. We always talked of this, you know, but we feared making such decisions, as parents, because we wanted more than an arranged marriage for our children." He stepped forward, and she threw her arms around him, hugging him tightly. "I am so happy for you, Grayson."

"Well, that is how all of this started. When I arrived home, a couple of weeks ago, I contacted Lord Satterfield. He was delighted and we are now ready to conclude the matter..." He allowed his voice to trail away.

"Is there some difficulty? Surely, there can be no objection?" his mother asked at once.

"No, nothing like that. The problem is..." He could hardly speak without laughing. His earlier concern about Susan kept him from enjoying his mother's dilemma. "Although

Susan knows she is to become betrothed, she does not know to whom. She became so upset with her father when she overheard him discussing it with her stepmother, she forgot to discover the name of her intended. She probably has expectations of the worst kind." He could not prevent a low guffaw.

"Oh, how cruel." His mother arched her brows in a look designed to chastise, but her quiet giggle gave her true feelings away. "However, it is amusing. Do you think, though, my dear, this deception could bring you home by Weeping Cross if she feels cornered and embarrassed? You must be very careful of her feelings in this, you know."

"I have thought of that, Mother, and you are right. I asked Lord Satterfield not to tell her."

"I beg your pardon? How will you marry her without her knowing your identity? I do not understand, son."

"I plan to *court* Susan. I want more than an arranged marriage, too."

"Grayson! I am delighted to hear that." She clasped her hands. "I cannot wait to welcome her into our family." Turning to Blaine, she said, "My dear, Grayson can be rather stubborn. I wish for grandchildren and have told him as much. I was not sure what might come of my actions, but I paraded as many mamas and their young daughters in front of my son as was possible—only those I could tolerate, you understand—although I still hoped... Oh, I am so delighted!"

Grayson chuckled. "I did not know. You outwitted me on this one, Mother. I was starting to avoid you."

"Oh... I could not be more pleased, my son. She is a beautiful young woman; Anna's little girl. Her mother would approve, I feel sure." Smiling more broadly still, she gripped Blaine's arm. "Shall we go into dinner?"

"Yes. I still have another matter to discuss. It is considerably more serious." Grayson walked alongside the couple to his mother's dining room. He never tired of the cheerful blue and white patterned wallpaper or the cherry-wood table and chairs. *The décor suits Mother.*

Grayson chewed a mouthful of ham, considering how to raise his concerns. "Mother, how well do you know Lady Prucilla Satterfield?" He turned to Lord Blaine. "And you, sir, do you know the present Countess?" The room was silent for some moments. At length, his mother put down her knife.

"Prucilla had her come-out at the same time as Anna and I did. We were not exactly friends. Her mama pushed her in Lord Satterfield's direction. He was a handsome young man —not yet a marquess, of course. As an earl, he was still highly sought after. My friend, Anna, caught his eye and they fell in love. Among the *ton*, that was unusual. It was not long before they were engaged and married. Prucilla was very spiteful when Anna married Lord Satterfield. She did some hateful things—she whispered horrible rumours to the *ton*, alleging that pregnancy forced the Satterfield nuptials, and asserting that Lord Satterfield was the father." His mother giggled. "Even today, the wrath that the old Marquess of Satterfield levelled upon her makes me laugh. He invited her and her mama to his son's engagement ball as his special guest and then tricked her into admitting loudly, in front of the biggest gossip in town, that she had invented the whole thing. As I recall, the entire dance floor became deathly quiet. She ran from the room in embarrass-ment, or so we all assumed. It surprised no one when she got her claws into Susan and Alex's father. I think he had the wool pulled over his eyes with her protestations that she was ashamed of her behaviour, and she fussed over his children."

Blaine took a sip of wine and placed his glass in front of him. He spoke in a sober tone. "Prucilla married Viscount Evans. He died some three or four years ago. My dear, am I recalling this correctly? I believe their only issue... a son... died in childbirth."

"Yes. While he was considerably older than Prucilla, the Viscount was a man who carried his age well. He had always appeared to be able-bodied and strong. Then he suddenly became ill and never recovered. It started as some sort of weakness, which continued to escalate until he died. The doctors could not agree about his malady. Some speculated he had contracted the Influenza, others that he had suffered some sort of poisoning. He left her well provided for, in any event."

"That is curious," Grayson mused aloud. "Would you not agree?"

"Grayson, what is on your mind? Why all this sudden interest in Lady Satterfield? She can be trouble. You should not stir up a hornet's nest, as they say."

"I am just being thorough, Mother. I do not plan to have anything to do with her." Shaking his head, he continued, "Young Lord Alexander is very sick and weakens by the day. His skin is translucent, and he is not allowed out. If I have the right of it, he is bled frequently, under direction of Lady Satterfield. It is my belief he has been. When Dr. Steth was called to the Winslow estate, he refused to bleed the boy and did so pointedly, in front of a room full of witnesses."

"I doubt that was well received," his mother ruminated out loud.

"No. I would have laughed but the young lord is very sick. I have invited father and son to Bellmane to ride with me." His mother clapped her hands together in approval.

"Wonderful! Anna was such a horsewoman. I have heard tell that Lady Susan rides well. You should invite her to join you. There can be no objection, with her father and brother present." She flicked an eyelid at him. "The young lord is bound to take to the pony. What a sterling idea!"

"You have both given me a great deal to think about. I hate to think the worst of someone, but the antipathy I felt when introduced to the current Lady Satterfield shocked me, and her manner towards the good doctor was disquieting." He looked down at his meal and pushed his beans about with his fork, taking a mouthful. "Mother, thank you so much for this hearty meal. I am touched you remembered my favourite dishes." He quirked a brow at her, noting that she glanced away.

"Of course, I do. I confess, I had a tiny favour to ask, but since you are to become affianced..." She waved her right hand nonchalantly. "... I find I no longer need to ask."

His mother faced him with a broad smile. It did not fool him. Blaine, he noticed, kept his head a little lower. They had been plotting something, that was obvious. His engagement with Lady Susan Winslow was timely. Grayson warmed to the thought of being married to Susan, sure that his life would not be dull.

———

Two days later—

Humming, Susan opened her eyes and spread her arms, absorbing the sun streaming in through the white lace curtains of her room. This would be a wondrous day. She could feel it.

Rose had already been in. The curtains had been pulled back and her cup of chocolate was sitting on a tray on the side-table with a scone. She needed to hurry but felt lazy. Her light-blue muslin dress lay neatly across her lavender cushioned chair, and the matching shoes were on the floor underneath. Noelle was curled up on her pillow and her black tail swatted Susan for disturbing her sleep. An abrupt, louder purr was soon followed by a chain of softer purrs, a signal she knew well. Noelle planned to remain sleeping.

Waking up today had been difficult. She had dreamed about Grayson, a dream in which he kissed her. He was no longer the loose-limbed fourteen-year-old she remembered. If not for the sun bursting into the room, she might still be enjoying that kiss. *This is twiddle-twaddle! We are friends, nothing more.* Her heart ignored her head, though. Each time she thought of the following day, a tickling feeling formed in the pit of her stomach. The kiss may be in her head, but the excursion was not.

This week she was going to see the Pavilion...*with Grayson.* She dared not hope too much. *Please let it be a glorious day.*

Grayson's sudden reappearance and the events of this weekend had caused her head to spin. It made it hard to keep her mind on what was real and what could be. Susan could not help herself. She had been visiting her mother's grave and had shared her concerns about Prucilla. She would swear she had heard her mother's voice answer those concerns, a voice she thought she had forgotten. Goose-flesh formed on her arms as she pondered. If not for that dratted tree falling on top of her, she might have had time for one more excursion with Grayson. Instead, she was cooped up here, recovering.

Susan could not fail to recall that the gentleman who had rescued her from certain death and disaster had been her dearest childhood friend. *How can I not be deliriously happy? I feel somehow that this is all connected by things I do not yet understand.*

She seized her blue muslin dress and hugged it close,

humming and dancing around her room, her eyes closed, until she bumped into the bed.

"Ha! I *am* sorry, Noelle. I know how much you value your sleep." She smiled impishly.

"Meowwww." Her companion rose and slunk down from her perch to stretch, her black paws working up and down on the pillow, accompanied by a strong feline hum.

"We need to busy ourselves, Noelle. Papa and Alex will be leaving for Bellmane shortly." She stamped her foot softly in mock anger. "I wish there was some way for me to go with them and not get into trouble. Come, help me think. I need to speak with Papa away from here. It is important."

The sleepy cat arched her back and walked to the edge of the bed nearest to Susan. Sitting down, Noelle washed the sleep from her eyes with her paws.

"How sweet you are, Noelle. Thank you for agreeing with me." Susan leaned down and kissed her pet on the nose. At that moment, the bedchamber door opened behind them and Alex marched into the room with Rose following.

"M'lady. I see by the gleam in your eyes you 'ave been dancing around the room with that dress. I fear ye are up to something." Her voice was filled with mirth even while she pretended irritation.

"I was merely dreaming, Rose. I promise."

"Susan, I get to ride a pony today! I have never been on an actual horse before," her brother interrupted.

Susan softly smiled at the blond, curly-headed boy. She wished he felt more himself.

"Are you scared, Alex?" She could tell he was not by the stubborn set of his chin.

"No, Sue-sue. I'm excited but a little scared I will not get to go. I heard Stepmother send a groom for a doctor. She told him not to bring Dr. Steth. I like Dr. Steth. He does not cut me. I think she does not want me to go today."

"Oh, do not worry, my dear. I know Papa will not allow you to miss this. He is going with you, you know—and from the looks of it, he is as excited as you!" She gently tapped her brother under the chin. She would make sure he got to go. She would watch over him and would do whatever she needed to protect him.

"Papa said he would let me ride on his horse with him to Bellmane. This will be beyond anything!"

Susan searched her brother's eyes, not missing the excitement radiating from them. This was the first time in months she had seen Alex excited about anything, and it cheered her heart. "You are in high ropes! It *will* be *beyond anything*, Alex." She clasped her gown to her chest in glee.

Rose extracted the dress from her damaging clutch. "Let me help you get dressed, m'lady." She turned to Alex and went on, "Young master, may we meet you downstairs in a few minutes? I need to help your sister to dress. I think I noticed Cook taking some lemon tarts from the oven this morning. If'n you were to pop down to the kitchen, she might be persuaded to let you try one. Are they not your favourite?"

"Ooh, yes! Papa is taking me to the stables, so we may be gone, Sue-sue, when you come down." With a wide grin, he scampered away.

Alex seemed to be a different child today. He had risen early and broken his fast with Papa. Then the two of them had planned to visit the stables, to pick out the gentlest mare for "practice riding." Although only six years old, her little brother continually showed the mettle of a leader. Papa had promised the mare to Alex if he enjoyed riding the pony at Bellmane.

Once dressed, Susan descended to the breakfast parlour to retrieve a book she favoured. She was leaving the room with the book when the Marchioness sauntered in for her morning ritual of drinking a cup of coffee and reading the morning newspaper, which her husband had delivered from town every day.

"Have you seen your brother?" she demanded. Her voice was full of irritation. Susan tried to hide a smile.

"Yes *Stepmama*. Have you been looking for him?" Susan asked innocently, before turning to leave. She knew better than to rub Prucilla's fur the wrong way, but the thought of the woman spoiling Alex's day infuriated her.

"Well, are you going to tell me where he is? I brought him porridge, and he was not in his room." The woman set down her cup, the sound forcing Susan to look around.

Susan faced the woman with the largest smile she could manage. "He broke his fast with Papa earlier, and then they went to the stables." Wheeling about to leave, she caught sight of Prucilla snatching up her coffee, the hot liquid splashing on her face and down the front of her morning dress.

"Damn!" The angered woman threw the cup, still filled with liquid, against the wall. The display was no surprise to Susan. Her stepmother knew dozens of words that ladies did not use. Tired of her tantrums, she stopped and briefly turned, noting Prucilla's startled look, while affecting a supercilious air. With the decorum of a queen, Susan exited the room.

Susan walked towards the front entrance, intent on joining her brother and father in the stables. She was almost at the door when she heard someone call to her.

"Lady Susan. Might I speak with you?"

Daniel was calling to her. *This is very unusual. Daniel rarely says a word.* Instinct told her it was important.

The footman caught up with her and motioned for her to follow him into her father's empty library.

"My lady, I would not trouble you with this, but I am

concerned." He held out a small bottle. "I found this in the carriage when I accompanied Lady Satterfield to town. She stopped at the pharmacy on North Street. I know I should say nothing, for it is none of my concern, but I see things."

"Have you spoken to Papa about this, Daniel?"

"No. I am not sure what to say to him. There may be nothing amiss, but I have seen her pour something into Lord Alex's food from a bottle much like this. I do not know what it is. But the young lord is so sick and seeming without explanation. I felt I should come forward."

Susan gasped. His revelation shocked her, as much as the risk he was taking in telling her what he had observed. Daniel had been with the family all Susan's life, but still she realized he risked his position with this accusation. He looked tired and worried.

"When did you see her pour something on his food? And what food was it?" Her mind was spinning, grasping at many possibilities.

"It was on his porridge, my lady. She brings it up to him, personally, every morning."

"I see. Thank you, Daniel, for informing me. You have always been so loyal to my family. I will deal with the matter now. You have an infirm sister, do you not? You must not jeopardize your position any further, although I very much appreciate your seeking me out." She normally would not speak so to a servant, but Daniel was more like family. He had grown up here, alongside her father. *It all makes sense. Alex has always hated hot cereal. This could be the cause of his illness.* Tears rimmed her eyes and dread rose in her heart.

"Yes, my lady."

"I need to reflect on what you have told me." She swallowed back her tears. It would never do to show her fears in front of the household. "Please inform me if anything else odd attracts your notice."

"Yes, my lady. A letter has arrived for your father. I can accompany you if you wish to speak with him immediately." He held out a stamped note from Bellmane.

"There is no need for you to trouble yourself. I am sure you have other duties to perform. I can take that to Papa. There can be no objection to my walking to the stables on such a fine morning." She prayed the missive was not to cancel the afternoon's entertainment.

"Thank you, my lady. I will inform you at once if I see anything else... out-of-the-way." He bowed and quietly left the room.

Susan remained, holding the note in one hand and the bottle in the other. The bottle was a clear blue-green and tiny —only about three inches tall, with a small cork stopper. There seemed to be some sort of powder residue in the bottom. Convinced that the bottle held the answer to what-ever ailed her brother, she needed to tell Papa... but would he believe her? She would have to mention Daniel to Papa, but would he believe him, and not tell Prucilla?

"This is dreadful. I must tell Papa what I know. Yet maybe I should see if I can find any other similar bottles in Prucilla's possession, first," she muttered. As she spoke, she glanced at the note. *Please do not let this be bad news.*

A ball of black fur meowed and moved between her legs, startling her. "Noelle. There you are, my sweet kitty. Your arrival is timely. Come with me to find Papa and Alex." Smiling at her pet, Susan stuffed the bottle into her pocket and reached down to pick up the humming ball of fur. She proceeded towards the stables, determined to speak to Papa before he left. Maybe there was still a way she might go with them? Certainly Grayson would not turn her away if she arrived with Papa and Alex. Her heart gave the familiar tick-ling feeling at the thought of him.

CHAPTER 6

*A*lton woke Grayson early. "My lord, I have ordered your bath. You asked that I not let you sleep late." He pulled the heavy navy curtains open, allowing bright sunlight to cascade through the glass panes.

"Ah, yes. Thank you, Alton." His valet was always prompt. Grayson wiped his eyes and swung his legs over the side of the bed onto the cold floor. He was sure he had just stepped on ice. *Where was the carpet?*

"Alton? The carpet is gone."

"Yes, my lord. It is my fault." He looked straight ahead, clearly embarrassed. "Some polish dropped on it yesterday and it is being cleaned. They assured me it would be here by this afternoon. I am deeply sorry for my clumsiness."

"Well, it makes more sense why the floor is cold this morning." He grinned. He had not even missed the rug when he fell into bed the night before. "Accidents happen, Alton. It sounds as though the carpet will survive, thanks to your quick action." His valet's face visibly relaxed into a slight smile.

Grayson had more important things to think about this

day. Steth would arrive in about an hour. Then Lord Satterfield and his son would be here this afternoon. Grayson wished he had thought to invite Susan, but he had been so startled over her brother's appearance, his concentration had lapsed. It had been far too late by the time his mother's comment had brought the notion to mind again. Susan would enjoy it, and he would dearly like to see her ride.

"Alton. I need your help in an urgent matter," he said, making a swift decision.

"Yes, my lord."

"I have a message to send to Satterfield Hall immediately." He went to his desk and scribbled a brief note, folded it and sealed it with red wax.

Alton left to dispatch a groom with the invitation for Lady Susan to join them. Grayson leaned back in the chair and smiled, hoping she would bring her horse and ride with them, glad to have remembered before it was too late. He hoped she would come; that she had suffered no adverse effects from the accident, which would prevent her from doing so.

His valet returned a short time later, and Grayson realized he was still sitting in his shirt. He had been lost in thought. The room was chilly, and the fire had just started crackling. It would be a few more minutes before there was any significant heat.

"Alton, do you recall where you placed my medical textbooks?"

"They are in your library, in the third bookcase from the door, and four shelves down, to the right of your desk, my lord. Would you like for me to fetch them?"

"No; no, that is… precisely… quite sufficient, thank you. I have need of them, but I will read them in the library." He shook his head and smiled. Alton's need for precision sometimes could be amusing. "I will have guests arriving today.

Could you have my bath brought up? I will break my fast in the library. Will you inform Cook?"

"Certainly, my lord. Here are your boots. I had the heels replaced. They had some worn spots on the edges. I will return to help you dress following your bath. Will there be anything else?"

"No. Thank you, Alton. I shall be but a few minutes."

Having lathered himself thoroughly with soap, Grayson enjoyed soaking in his copper tub filled with hot water. *It feels good to relax and think. Steth should be here soon, so I need to go downstairs and look up a few things.*

Alex Winslow had looked in a bad way yesterday. *If my suspicions are correct, we need to act quickly. This airing should help improve his mood, at the very least.* He thought about the orangery at the back of the house. Somewhere he had read that the juicy fruit might help with the effects of arsenic. There had been observations and speculation, but nothing, to his knowledge, had been proved for certain. *It is worth a try.*

The water had cooled, so Grayson swiftly dipped his head to give his hair a final rinsing before getting out to get dressed.

Shortly afterwards, he was settled in his library behind a desk cluttered with thick books. Scores of pages were bent back for reference, with book stacked upon book. He moved his cold plate of fruit and cheese to an occasional table next to him.

He looked up when Rudolph, the family butler, appeared at the door.

"My lord, you have visitors." He walked across the room, carrying a small salver on which lay a pair of visiting cards.

The man's loud voice boomed across the room. Grayson suspected that the butler was going deaf, but he had been with the family so long, Grayson would not replace him. When that time came, retirement would be Rudolph's decision. The man had never married; the Harding family was his family. Grayson would pension him handsomely when that time came.

"His Grace, the Duke of Hollingbury is here, as well as Dr. Steth."

"Ah, yes. Thank you, Rudolph. I have been expecting Dr. Steth." He rose from his desk in time to greet his best friend, Cooper Haroldson, the Duke of Hollingbury, who had followed Rudolph into the library.

"Your Grace." Grayson extended his hand and shook his friend's hand. The two of them embraced, slapping each other's backs. "This is a pleasant surprise! It has been months. How was your trip to France?"

"It was good. A little work, a little play." He chuckled.

"Cooper, it is good to see you again. You have timed your arrival to perfection. I am to be betrothed… to Lady Susan Winslow and will tell you all about it later—there is much to share. However, I seem to have got myself in a bit of a predicament, though." He smiled sheepishly. "The lady is unaware they betrothed her to me."

"You were never one to be a dull dog, were you, Grayson? So, it is a *secret* engagement, even from the woman? I want to hear all about this one." He dropped into a chair in front of Grayson's desk and slapped his knee. "Go on."

"Later. I have something to take care of and you can help with that as well. First, let me have Steth shown in." He pulled the bell for Rudolph, who appeared within moments.

"Rudolph, please ask Dr. Steth to join us." Rudolph nodded. "Very good, my lord."

Cooper waited until Rudolph was out of sight. "I told him to follow me, but he refused. That butler of yours gave us both the *eye*," he whispered loudly.

The two of them laughed uproariously.

"Ah, yes. Rudolph's *eye.* That always means to *move at your peril.* Your best ducal glare cannot compare!"

Grayson poured Cooper a tumbler of brandy and handed it to him.

"Thank you. Your French brandy is the best, my friend."

Rudolph returned to the room minutes later with Dr. Steth. "Cooper, do you remember Doctor Joseph Steth? Steth, do you recall His Grace?"

The doctor set his bag down beside the door, bowed and then extended his hand, shaking those of both men.

"I do, my lord. It is nice to see you again, your Grace."

"Please, Doctor, do not stand upon ceremony when we are among friends. Call me Haroldson. I cannot recall what you called me when we were at university."

"Very good, sir, if you so wish. Might I request you do the same?"

"Indeed." Cooper inclined his head in acknowledgement.

"Now that the introductions are out of the way," Grayson interposed, "I would like to talk about something which worries me greatly. Steth, I perceived we might agree with this. Lady Susan Winslow is to become my wife. At least, I hope she will agree to do so. We were close as children, yet when I left years ago, for some reason unknown to me, we could not communicate. It seems that ladies do not 'associate' with young boys after a certain age." He stopped for a second to think about that, but shook his head in feigned confusion.

"Gray... tell us something we do not know." Cooper took a swallow and grinned. "It would have been unseemly."

"Yes, well, she was my best friend, and we had shared many adventures and childhood secrets. The two of us had been together since being in leading-strings. Ahem." He paused and also refreshed himself from his glass. "Anyway, I came home from my recent assignments, and went to visit her father. I asked for her hand—and we have a betrothal agreement..."

"... which she knows nothing about," finished Cooper.

"That explains your presence in the household... and your interest in Lord Alexander," Steth continued.

"I do plan to court her. I thought better of my methods and have asked her father not to tell her of the agreement. Susan has a mind of her own. She can become angry and irascible if provoked and can be stubborn to the point of ridiculousness. I need to win her. The woman has consumed my thoughts and my heart for years. She is aware there is an agreement but flew into such a pucker, she left the house and does not know with whom they have made the agreement."

"Wait. This is marvellous," Cooper interrupted. "She does not know you are the one? Oh, *this* will be hugely entertaining. I wager you a crown she is imagining a toothless old man with a paunch the size of dear Prinny's!" He roared with laughter.

"Yes, there is that." Grayson had already berated himself soundly over the agreement, but it was too late. The settlements were drawn up and ready for signatures. He wanted to win her hand first, but a nagging feeling kept telling him to push on with it. He had a face for that nagging feeling—Lady Prucilla Satterfield. "Steth, I spent time this morning reading and re-reading my books and I kept coming back to the possibility of arsenic."

"The Poison of Kings?" Cooper looked stunned.

"Yes. I suppose it could be accidental, but my instincts are telling me otherwise." He brought out another glass and the brandy and poured a generous amount for the doctor.

"I apologize, gentlemen, but I will have to leave soon." Steth tossed back half the contents and placed his glass down, waving away the proffered decanter. "I have a woman who is about to deliver her first child, and I promised I would call in on her today. I am, however, in accordance with you, Harding. My thoughts have been travelling along the same path."

"My fear is how she is she doing this. Via the boy's food?" Steth took another mouthful of brandy. "That will be hard to prove. The young lord is getting worse. To my shame, I had suspected none of this until yesterday, when she behaved so strangely. She was almost *desperate*, insisting I bleed the boy. I refused. Many doctors still believe in bleeding, but in my view, it would make matters worse. The boy is so thin; his skin is translucent, for God's sake."

"That shocked me," Grayson uttered.

Steth nodded. "I have made a few discreet enquiries, and she has used several of the doctors in the area. If they refuse, she threatens them, as she did me. She is a powerful woman, married to the Marquess of Satterfield. It is hard for humble practitioners to gainsay her. I fear the child will not survive much longer. He has a terrible stomach. The symptoms of arsenic poisoning mimic cholera, among other things. It makes it very hard to determine."

"I think I should hire a Bow Street Runner. He can at least look into the matter in an official capacity: discover potential sources of the drug and question those who may have supplied it. Perhaps fortune will shine on us." Grayson stood up and walked to the window, and stared down at the perfectly groomed gardens below. *Susan will probably add more roses.* "I have been looking into the Marchioness' background. I spoke with my mother yesterday evening."

"How is Lady Harding? I have it in mind to pay her a visit."

"Yes, Cooper, she would like that. Would you believe, she now has a beau? Ambrose, Viscount Blaine."

"Ah. Good man, Blaine." The Duke nodded.

Steth concurred.

"Anyway, to continue, Mother told me about the current Lady Satterfield's previous husband. He became very ill and ultimately died, although he was a strong, virile man despite being older than she."

Cooper scratched his head and leaned back. "I had heard rumblings from other officers while I was in the navy, but nothing was proven. I will call in a runner. I know the perfect one for this job. He has done a little work for me recently. Perhaps Lady Satterfield will show her hand, so to speak, if she indeed has one in this illness. Viscount Evans was a friend of my father's. They did not always travel in the same circles, but they were good friends from childhood. If we find the Marchioness is involved in the boy's sickness, I will appeal to the Prince Regent."

The Duke arched his brows, looking pointedly from Grayson to the doctor before continuing. "I can guess at a possible motive with Viscount Evans, although there was no evidence. She became a very wealthy widow who could move within fashionable Society to suit her whim. What I do not understand is why she would target a child. It makes no sense to me. He is but a *boy*."

"You have the right of it, Cooper. Since Susan will be my wife, I feel a certain responsibility to do what I can to help her brother—and also to keep her safe."

Before either of the other men could respond, a polite cough from the doorway brought an end to the conversation.

"Yes, Rudolph?"

"My lord, the Marquess of Satterfield, his son, Lord Alexander Winslow, and his daughter, Lady Susan Winslow, have arrived. I have placed them in the red and gold drawing room. The greying butler bowed and left the room.

Steth turned to Cooper and Grayson. "I must leave now, gentlemen. Do, please, keep me informed of any findings. I feel as though we are stabbing at moths in the dark, but the hairs on the back of my neck have been right too many times to ignore. Your Grace—Haroldson—it was good to see you again. Thank you for including me in your plans, Harding. I rarely imbibe this early," he smiled, "but when presented with such a delicious choice in brandy, I could not refuse." Grinning, he tipped his head in acknowledgement. "The brandy was most welcome."

"I must leave as well." Cooper stood up and walked around his chair to where Steth stood.

Grayson shook his friends' hands and walked them to the front entrance. His guests were in the drawing room. *She was here!*

CHAPTER 7

Susan could not believe that in a few minutes she would be at Bellmane. Providence must be watching over her because she had barely wished it, and then a note had arrived, inviting her to accompany Papa and Alex.

Oddly, Rose must have expected it too, for her navy-blue riding habit of fine merino wool was waiting for her on the end of her bed. Sometimes the woman had an uncanny knack of sensing things were about to happen. Susan had long since stopped puzzling over how her maid could have known. She recalled Mama telling her of being startled by Rose's eerie ability to foresee future events. It was better to accept it than to worry about how it was possible.

She looked out the window of the carriage and saw an older man approaching them. "Papa? There is a man on horseback approaching us."

"There is? Oh dear, I forgot about Lord Aldrington's visit." He sighed. We have business to conclude. Let me apologize." He tapped the roof of the carriage to stop it. "I will leave the carriage but will be right back." The marquess exited the carriage and waved at Aldrington, who immediately stopped to talk.

Susan casually peered outside her window and watched the two men carry on an animated conversation. *The Earl of Aldrington has always made me feel odd in his presence*, she thought, distracted. His fat lips always throw spittle as talks. And he has the worse breath. She observed her father take a step back and laughed. It was the way he constantly stared at her in his company that gave her the most unease. *It is as if I am the roast duck on a menu.* A sudden shudder overtook her.

"Who is that man, Susan?" Alex's face was glued to the window, watching his parent.

"It seems to be a man that Papa had an appointment with but forgot when he made plans for our visit to Bellmane. I am certain he will be quick." She leaned back in the squabs. Oh, no! Father said he was concluding the betrothal business this week. Surely, he would not consider Lord Aldrington! Bile rose in her throat, but she swallowed, forcing it back.

"Do you think he will come with us? He seems displeased with Papa." Alex's innocent question only added to her distress.

"No. Surely he will not." Her tone was abrupt. "I did not mean to sound so short, Alex. I simply mean, he most likely will meet him at home later."

Oh no, no, no... not Lord Aldrington. Should she ask? Papa had not considered her feelings in this... arrangement. She would have to decide things soon. Her time was running out. And she could not bear to marry the Earl of Aldrington! *No. Today is Alex's day. I will not spoil that with what would turn into a distasteful argument with Papa.* She would pray and hope Papa was not tying her to that dreadful man! And besides, whatever he decided, she had already decided... she might just leave. She was not sure... but it was a strong 'maybe.' However, if she married him, she could bring Alex with her away from Prucilla. That was something she would consider. And should. But to Lord Aldrington? She did not know if she could do that, even for Alex.

Her father returned to the carriage, and the three of them continued towards Bellmane. Any thought of conversation Susan might have had before the interruption was squelched now. She had too much on her mind.

The family carriage turned onto the drive leading to the three-storeyed baroque manor. Two curved stairways led to the bowed centre front of the house, which was framed by an arched stone portico. Sashed windows with oak shutters lined the first two storeys. Small, shutterless windows wove themselves between arabesques and round medallions on the third story.

As they pulled up before the house, a massive oak door opened, and a tall, if slightly stooping, butler stepped out. Having welcomed them into the house, he showed them into the drawing room. She recognized Rudolph. He had become more bent than he had been years ago, but his dark features had gained only small amounts of grey. She heard Dr. Steth and another voice she did not recognize speaking in the hall. They thanked Rudolph for retrieving their coats, their voices then becoming muffled as they presumably moved towards the entrance.

Susan looked about the drawing room, which had not changed a great deal, either. Red and gold damask wallpaper lined the walls. A yellow damask sofa rested between two large windows and was framed by two black lacquered chairs. An oak-mantled fireplace dominated the wall to the left, and a pianoforte was placed diagonally to the right rear window. The room evoked memories. The last time she had been in this room, her mother had been sitting next to her. Rather than making her sad, the thought of her mother buoyed her spirits. Susan recalled playing *Greensleeves* for both mothers—her own dear mama and Lady Harding—during one particular visit. Grayson had complimented her on her ability to play, which had made her feel wonderful. *I cannot wait to see him.*

Dr. Steth had visited yesterday and pronounced her fit to engage in activities again. She had been free of the headache and all signs of dizziness for two days.

"Papa, how big do you think the pony will be?" Alex's question to her father brought her out of her reverie.

"He will be a perfect size for you, my son, of that I am sure. One day, you know, you will grow up and be able to ride a big horse. It is very kind of Lord Harding to allow you to ride his young pony today."

"I am very excited, Papa. I have always wanted to ride." Her brother screwed up his face and pulled on her father's coat, looking up at him. "Do you think Stepmother will still be angry with me for coming here, when we get back home?"

"Son, I do not think she was angry with you. I believe she was worried about you. You do not need to fret about such things."

"She told me she did not like Dr. Steth and was getting a new doctor to see me this morning. I do not want to be cut any more. Please, Papa."

Susan had it in mind to discuss this with Papa, but it was better coming directly from Alex. She was unused to her brother speaking up about his stepmother; he was frightened of her. She looked at her papa, whose face had grown mottled, pale with splotches of red.

"Did you know anything about a different doctor being called today?" His tone was clearly one of displeasure.

"Yes, Papa, but only after Alex told me. We left to come here shortly after it came to my attention, and I have not had the chance to speak with you. I had gone to the breakfast parlour this morning to retrieve a book I left yesterday.

Prucilla arrived as I was leaving. She took one of her miffs, and I am afraid we lost a dish or two."

"You broke a dish?"

"No, Papa. Prucilla threw some at the wall after I left the room," she whispered to him, while her brother admired a small music box on a side-table.

"I see." He lifted Alex and pointed through a window which overlooked the side of the house. "Lord Harding has a large, handsome stable, my boy. It looks like this house, only much smaller. I believe you can see it beyond the shrubbery. You may even see some horses in the yard, if you look hard enough."

"Really?" Alex's excitement was palpable. Father put him down and Alex leaned against one of the floor-to-ceiling windows, pushing his face to the glass and watched. "I *do* see horses in the far pasture, Papa." He was clearly fascinated. The rascal kept his face glued to the window.

Walking back to Susan, her father sat down and then leaned over. "Daughter, I should not ask this of you," he whispered, "but I wish you to stay close to your brother. There are some matters I need to take care of."

Perhaps there is more to Prucilla's temper this morning. No, she was irritated because Alex was sitting with me. I know it. "All right, Papa." She had already planned to stay near him, but her father's words made her feel slightly shaken.

Her brother was so excited; she could not bear to have his day ruined by Prucilla. "Alex, you will have such fun today, I know. We shall not miss a moment of it." Susan playfully ruffled her brother's hair and then bent down and kissed him on the top of his head.

The door opened, and Grayson walked in. "Good afternoon, Lord Satterfield, Lady Susan. Greetings, Lord Alex! I have some exciting news for you. A beautiful black pony with white feet is waiting at the stables to meet you!"

My goodness, he has gotten so handsome. I will focus on having fun with Alex, Papa, and Grayson today, nothing else. Susan realized she was staring at her friend and blushed, hoping he had not seen her.

"A black pony! Alex, the pony you read about yesterday was black! Susan returned her attention to her little brother.

"Father showed me where your stables are, but I did not see a pony. I saw a groom leading a big red horse." The little boy jumped up and down. Smiling, their father raised one eyebrow, which served to plant her brother's feet but did not squelch his enthusiasm.

"Oh, he is there," Grayson replied cheerfully. "The groom is readying him for you. The red horse is going to the smith to be shod." He turned to Lord Satterfield and Susan. "This could not be better weather. It is crisp but not too cold, just as I prefer it." As he spoke, he looked over at her and smiled.

"It should put some colour into his cheeks," Papa added, patting his son's back. "Alex is excited, to say the least. I was considering buying him a horse when he became ill. I am glad Dr. Steth is fairly progressive in his thinking and willing to give the outdoors a try, in moderation."

Yes, away from Prucilla. Susan intended to make sure Alex joined her every morning to break his fast. There would be no more porridge upstairs, if she had anything to do with it. She determined to tell Papa what Daniel had told her as soon as she had the chance, and swore to herself she would keep her eyes on Alex whenever food or drink was served. Somehow Prucilla was everywhere. Why would Prucilla hurt her brother? And why was she trying to find a different doctor for him? She needed no superior intellect to recognize that both her father and her brother liked Dr. Steth very much. Prucilla's behaviour made little sense, except that the woman had a black heart.

The minute Grayson had walked into the room, the

fragrance of Bay Rum he favoured had wafted to her nose, and her heart had done a happy flip. She itched to rise and go to him, but that would have been most improper. Instead, she contented herself with admiring his impeccable dress. Over a pair of buckskin breeches and gleaming top-boots, he wore a subdued tan waistcoat and brown coat. His perfectly-styled neckcloth and simple gold pin were quite perfect. Tied in a queue, his brown curls touched the shoulder of his coat. Susan knew his valet took great pride in his master's dress, and she felt her neck heat as she appreciated the servant's efforts. Grayson's kindness towards Alex warmed her heart; unbidden, it gave another leap. Courtesy dictated today's visit could last only a few hours, yet the smallest amount of time with Grayson made her happy. It had always been so.

"Susan, I am glad you could come today. Almost too late, I realized I had not included you in the invitation, not knowing how you would feel after the accident. You look to have recovered well."

"Yes, I am quite well again. Thank you. The megrim has been gone some two days, and I suffered no other ill effects. "

"That is excellent news." He smiled at her, and it lit up her soul. "If I recall, you were a very able horsewoman. I have no doubts that skill has only improved."

"Papa relented to my coming if I promised not to *ride neck or nothing on a cock-horse!* He allowed me to bring Smudge, though."

"You had just bought Smudge, I seem to remember, when I left. Do you ride him often?"

"As often as I can. I am hoping Alex will learn quickly so the three of us can ride together."

Grayson raised a brow at her remark, and she realized her omission at once. "Prucilla dislikes riding, so Papa and I frequently go about the estate together. It will be delightful to have Alex join us," she added smoothly.

"Yes, Lady Satterfield does not appreciate horseflesh or the pleasures of such exercise. She prefers the carriage and well uses it." Lord Satterfield spoke in a low tone.

Susan noticed there was still an edge to Papa's voice when he regarded Prucilla. *I must have missed something.* Perhaps here was her opportunity to approach Papa regarding Alex. Regardless of any other considerations, he must be told what Daniel saw, and soon.

"The pony should be saddled by now. Shall we?" Grayson ushered them all to the door. "Alex, I have not yet named the pony, and would like very much for you to assist me in that."

"Oh, yes indeed, sir! I have been thinking of names... but I want to meet him first. Papa said the right name will come to me when I know the horse." Her brother was bubbling with excitement and anticipation.

They followed Grayson to the stables, which almost mirrored a smaller version of his home. The stables were easily accessible from the main house via the rear exit to the garden. Susan lamented to herself that she would love to ride Smudge on a day like today and give her horse his head across the fields, but thoughts of the grievous headache she had recently endured tempered that desire. Riding at a gentle pace with her, Papa and Alex would do nicely. It had been two days since the headache had prostrated her, and she never wished for that again!

The groom met them as soon as they approached the stable yard. "The little 'orse be ready, my lord."

"Marvellous." Grayson turned to Alex. "Shall we meet him?"

"Oh, yes!" Alex was almost hopping on one foot, he was so excited. They walked inside the long building. Within a stall, a small horse waited, nuzzling at the last wisps of hay in the manger.

Just as he had described, the little pony was black, with

white patches like socks on each of his four legs and a white star on his forehead in the shape of a crescent moon.

Alex extended his hand and cautiously stroked the animal's nose. The pony turned to look at the boy. Staring in admiration at the pony's face, he commented on the star.

"It is so pretty," he declared. "'Tis a moon!"

Susan noted the thoughtful approach her brother was making and watched him bite his lower lip as he took in the pony's appearance.

"What do you think of *Night Star*, sir?" He posed his question to Grayson, his hands clasped together.

"I like it!" Grayson exclaimed, matching her brother's enthusiasm. "The shape of his star—that is what the moon is called, no matter its form—makes him rather unique. *Night Star*," he said with emphasis.

"Son, that is a splendid name," her father added. "It has a pleasant ring to it and foretells a future of leadership."

"I really do like it!" Grayson's excitement was palpable. He patted the pony's head lightly. "Night Star, are you ready to show us what you can do?" He turned to Alex. "Are you ready to learn to ride, sir?"

"Oh, yes, sir! Papa, is it all right for me to learn now?"

"Of course, my son. You and the pony need to get to know each other first, though."

Grayson pulled a carrot from his pocket, cut it in half with a pocket knife, and then spoke instructions to her brother in calm, easy tones.

"Alex, hold the carrot up to Night Star. Put it on your open palm and let him come to you and take it. Keep your hand flat, now."

Her brother's face lit up when the pony gently took first one half of the carrot and then the other, chewing noisily. Soon he was stroking its face and mane and getting closer.

This was the Alex Susan was used to seeing, bright-eyed, cheery, and *full* of vivacity.

She nibbled her lower lip, wondering where the best place would be to speak with Papa. They rarely had privacy, except on their rides across the estate. Prucilla seemed to insert herself into any occasion. Reaching into her pocket, she fingered the bottle Daniel had given her. She had brought it with her because she had not had time to find a good hiding place in her room. Besides, she wanted to have it when she spoke to Papa. Perhaps today would be a good time —once Alex was riding and enjoying himself. She did not want to interfere with that because it was almost as important to her as discovering what ailed him.

Content with her decision, Susan relaxed a little and turned her attention to her brother. Before long, he was riding Night Star, being led around the stable yard by the groom.

"Look, Papa! Look, Sue-Sue! I'm riding him." The little boy bobbed past them on the pony's back, his smile stretching from ear to ear.

"Alex, you look to have a natural affinity in the saddle." Her father smiled broadly and leaned towards his son and gently hugged him.

She watched Grayson step towards her father and speak in low tones. It was obviously something not intended for her ears. Irritation flared. What in the world could the two of them have to talk about? He had not been home very long. She abhorred the low practice of eavesdropping, but edged closer to the men.

Grayson was pleased the day was going so well. Susan had come, and he hoped he might contrive a few minutes alone with her. Alex was riding the pony and had even chosen a good name for him. Night Star was an excellent name for the pony. He had named Blacklock for an unusual, long black lock of mane which flopped down and curled over a large white star on his forehead. *How ironic*, Grayson thought.

The boy was doing wonderfully, and there was pink in his cheeks. Of course, the brisk air had much to do with that, but he noticed Alex had energy today, something he had not observed earlier. That was good. He wondered how much he could tell Lord Satterfield of his conversation with Steth. The boy needed to be watched every moment, if his suspicions were correct, or the situation could become grave. After deliberating for some minutes, he gave in to the need to speak with Satterfield. Keeping his request light, he asked if he could see his lordship before the family left. Now he needed to consider *how* to speak to the Marquess.

He did not miss Susan sidling closer, or her interest in their conversation, and he smiled to himself. Although she could be keen about things, she was definitely not retiring. Oddly, he liked the inquisitive side of her nature. Not much had changed about her–except for physically. She had transformed into a diamond of the first water, and he was glad she would not need a Season, as her father put it. She looked gorgeous in the deep blue riding habit she wore. His body was increasingly aware of her. And her nature had not changed. She was still adventurous and could be hoydenish when she felt left out of events. Perhaps today would not be a good day… He needed to be careful in his approach, for he expected Lord Satterfield might become overwrought with the conversation. Alex's health concerned him greatly.

Alex was doing very well with Night Star. Grayson suggested they move beyond the stables. Maybe a short outing would give him a suitable opportunity. "Lord Satterfield, I think Alex could be ready for bigger things. It occurs to me an excursion to our chapel would be short enough for him to gain confidence. He may build his distances later."

"That is an excellent idea, my boy. You have already given us so much today, I doubt I shall ever be able to repay your kindness. However, if I do not miss my guess, Susan is champing at the bit to ride Smudge. Alex will go anywhere his sister does. You need have no fear on that score. You will receive no complaint either. I have little doubt he will find it an adventure!"

Grayson walked across to where Susan was standing, watching her brother. "Are you game to press on and take Alex on a short ride? I will hold onto his pony."

"I think we would love to!" She gave him an enormous smile, her eyes luminous with unshed tears. It almost undid him.

"Fortunately, unlike many stallions, Blacklock has no objection to ponies. Nevertheless, I shall take good care he minds his manners in front of Alex." He laughed. "I do not want to overstretch Alex today, but I wish to give him enough taste for the sport to keep him trying for more. I suspect in a few weeks' time, he will be a horseman."

The ride to the chapel and back went by too quickly for Grayson's liking. The chapel stood behind a pond just to the right of the stables, protected by a small grove of lush trees. It was close enough to both the house and stables to readily see. But he realized the importance of not taxing Alex beyond his capabilities, so kept the excursion short. In all likelihood, Alex would pay for today with fatigue later. Perhaps, Grayson mused, he should speak with Lord Satterfield and prepare him for his son's probable fatigue. Grayson handed

Night Star's leading rein to the groom riding behind. "Take this and keep the pony to this steady pace."

"Yes, my lord," the groom responded, adding with unaccustomed enthusiasm, "He has certainly taken to the pony, eh? Already he rides like he was born to the saddle."

Grayson liked his groom. Many a long year before, the man had turned a blind eye to certain youthful peccadilloes by his young master.

"He does at that," he replied with a grin. "See he comes to no harm." He handed over the leading rein and trotted the couple of horse lengths to join Lord Satterfield, who was riding ahead.

"Lord Satterfield, a word with you, if you will?"

"Certainly." The older man drew rein and fell into line beside him. Grayson noticed Susan edged her mount slightly forward and subtly angled her body in their direction. He could not prevent a soft chuckle from escaping.

"Lord Satterfield, I fear there is no easy way to say what I must." After the tiniest of pauses, he ploughed on. Surely it was better not to beat about the bush? "I suspect the circumstances of Alex's illness and have checked my own sources to confirm or deny my conjectures. I have also spoken with Dr. Steth."

"You think you know what ails my son? Speak, boy."

Grayson took a fortifying breath. "My lord, it would not be uncommon to see these symptoms with an overdose of arsenic." He exhaled slowly and watched Satterfield's face as conflicting emotions of surprise, fear, and anger crossed his features.

"How?" The single word held a gamut of fiercely contained feeling.

"I cannot be sure, of course. As I am sure you know, arsenic is easy to get. There are many processes in which arsenic is used.

Is this the first time he has been sick like this? Currently, there has been speculation in the medical journals about the use of arsenic in green fabrics, wallpaper, and even sweetmeats. There is a genuine fear it is poisoning people by leaching into the air. I am sure much has to be learned about this, but I vetoed Mother's notion to use green fabric decorations in our town house."

"I want to be angry with you for suggesting this." Satterfield spoke in an agitated tone. "Yet I have pondered the same over the last few days. Alex has always been a robust and energetic child. He was hardly ever sick. Now he is so weak; his health consumes me with worry. I do not know where he could get this arsenic from, if that is the cause. It could not be intentional..." His voice broke. "Prucilla just had green curtains hung in the nursery."

Grayson bit his tongue in an effort to temper his reply. This could be entirely coincidental. He needed to tread carefully.

"Lord Satterfield, there is no certainty with the green, only speculation based on cause and effect, but I would encourage you to hang a different colour curtain. Young Alex seems to have enjoyed today's outing. Would you be amenable to bringing him a few times a week to allow him to ride the pony? I think the pony would benefit from the attachment, and Alex seems to enjoy himself tremendously. They may be of mutual benefit to each other."

Too late, Grayson realized Susan had joined them and that she had overheard a considerable part of the conversation. The questions would come soon enough, of that he was certain.

"Why do we not meet in the drawing room on our return and discuss this more? I will have Cook take Alex into the kitchen for some of her vanilla ice-cream. It is the stuff of small boys' dreams—and not so small boys too!"

"Yes, I think my son has done enough riding for today. He will much enjoy the ice-cream."

"Most certainly. Shall we?" The small group left the horses at the stables and walked towards the back entrance of the house. Alex was beaming with pride in his accomplishment, and half walked, half skipped to the house.

Grayson walked close to Susan, and she nudged him gently on the arm.

"Why do you suspect arsenic?"

"The better question is, how did you hear what I said?"

She blushed hotly. "I may have something to add."

He looked at her, searching her upturned face. *Does she know something?* Abruptly, she looked away.

"Would you feel comfortable telling me what that is?"

"I would." She glanced at her father, walking ahead with Alex. "This morning, our footman, Daniel, came to me. He told me that he had seen Stepmother put something in Alex's porridge. Apparently, she brings him gruel daily, in his room. Alex hates porridge but is afraid of Prucilla. She always behaves in a very caring manner when she is in our company. But something has changed. I do not know how long he has been eating porridge and have not asked him because there has been little opportunity. However, I believe Alex would be quite clear about it if you inquired of him. He is remarkably astute about such things for one so young." She exhaled slowly. "This morning, Prucilla came to the dining room, asking for Alex's whereabouts. She became furious when I responded he had broken his fast earlier, with me, and that he was in the stables with Papa. Prucilla held a bowl in her hand—probably porridge she had been taking to him. She became enraged. When I left the room, she threw dishes at the wall and swore in a most indecorous manner."

"This behaviour is extraordinary. Would you object if I accompanied you when you tell your father about this?"

"No, Grayson. I would appreciate your presence."

"In that case, I will send Alex to the kitchen with Cook for ice cream or one of her famous lemon tarts. Please join me in my library when we reach the house.

The Marquess did not object to meeting in the library, especially since Alex was enjoying a lemon tart in the kitchen. Cook liked children and had at once taken the boy under her wing. A few minutes later, Grayson opened the door to his library and saw Susan sitting on the burgundy velvet window seat.

"Daughter, I am startled to see you here," Satterfield said with a frown. "Is there something wrong?"

She wrung her hands. "Yes, Papa. As I mentioned earlier, I had a rather disagreeable experience this morning. There is more to tell before we go home."

"First, let me show you something." She fished into her pocket and pulled out a small bottle. The Marquess took the small blue-green bottle and rolled it about in his hand.

"It's a small bottle. I cannot follow." He looked at his daughter and then at Grayson, but said nothing.

"Father, this morning Daniel asked to speak with me." She looked up over at her friend. "You should know, Grayson, that Daniel looks upon our family as his own. He has been a part of our household forever, and I trust him."

"Daughter, what does this have to do with that bottle?"

Susan took a deep breath. "Daniel told me that recently he saw Prucilla sprinkle something from a bottle into a bowl of porridge she was taking to Alex. On the heels of what happened this morning, I thought it important." Susan smoothed her habit with a thoughtful expression and then continued, "He found this bottle in the carriage after Prucilla had returned from a visit to the chemist in town. It still has some powder residue from its former contents. "

Grayson observed Lord Satterfield's face grow pale. "Sir,

we are clearly speculating on things we need to know more about. I felt it was important I apprised you of this before you returned home. If you have no objections, I would like to discuss this with Dr. Steth. We cannot be sure this is what ails Alex and should be cautious about how we handle this new information. It would be helpful to find out if the Countess does indeed have arsenic in her possession—which would be rather odd."

"Do you think my son is being deliberately poisoned by... *my wife*? This seems inconceivable." His voice trembled slightly.

"Lord Satterfield, we do not know that. You must agree, though, that this information gives us even more reason to be concerned. I would like to speak to Dr. Steth... and I have a friend who can find out the purchase made at the dispensary."

"I cannot believe this of my wife, and I cannot fathom a reason for her to do such a thing. While you have not accused her, you have given me information that begs me to do it. I must protect my son, yet I feel I should keep quiet until I hear further information from you, Harding. I implore you to get back with me as quickly as possible."

"My only concern is your son's well-being, my lord." Grayson strongly suspected the woman was poisoning her stepson with his food. *But why?*

CHAPTER 8

*I*t was eight o'clock. Grayson would be here in two hours. It had been three days since she had seen him, but today was their promised outing. Susan needed to hurry. One thing she remembered about Grayson was that he was always on time.

"Come along, Noelle, we need to hasten." Her cat stretched and meowed, making sure that Susan knew it was inconvenient to move at this hour. Susan pulled the bell-rope beside her bed.

A couple of minutes later, Rose entered the bedchamber. "'Tis a big day, my lady, and time you dressed." She held a small silver tray and pushed it forward on the table. I brought this for you. I didn't think how you would break your fast."

"How thoughtful, Rose. Thank you. *Oh… you brought a* bowl of milk for Noelle." Sitting on the bed, she patted her side. "Come here, my sweet girl. Look what Rose has brought for you."

"Meooow." Noelle glided slowly towards the bowl of milk and began lapping.

"I will leave you to enjoy your toast and will return to help you dress in half an hour."

"Thank you, Rose. My lavender floral merino wool is a perfect choice. The weather could turn inclement."

"M'lady, lavender was your mother's favourite colour for you because it brings out the amber of your eyes, and the fairness of your hair and skin. I thought it would be the right dress for your expedition."

"Before you leave, there is one more thing I wish you to do. Could you ring for a tray for Alex, please? I promised we could break our fast together. Please make sure he rises and comes to my room."

"I believe he is breaking his fast with your father this morning, m'lady."

"Oh, I see. Is my stepmother there as well?"

"No, m'lady. The Countess has gone to town, it seems, to do some shopping. She took a footman."

Susan swallowed her surprise. "Do you know which foot-man?" she asked airily.

"Daniel, I think, m'lady. Is it important?"

Daniel will be more observant of her activities, she thought. "No, I do not suppose so." It was best to keep Rose in the dark about her suspicions, because the maid was not good at keeping secrets.

"I am merely appreciative of her absence," Susan responded in a neutral tone. She thought for a moment, hoping her face remained devoid of emotion.

"Your papa and Alex were talking about going to Bell-mane to ride again today. Your brother talks non-stop about that pony… Night Star, is it, he calls him? The fresh air is helping, I believe. He is looking a better colour."

"I have noticed it as well. I hope it continues. That will be all, Rose."

Alex is with Papa. Papa has been spending much more time

with Alex since we returned from Bellmane the other day. He is taking our fears seriously.

During the last three days, when her father had been busy, Susan had spent time with her brother, especially during meals or when a nuncheon was served. On those occasions she encountered Prucilla, the atmosphere was tense. While she tried to reason why the woman would commit such infamy, she did not think her stepmother suspected anything. Susan avoided Prucilla whenever possible, because she had noticed how much the disquiet between them upset her father.

A little over half an hour later, Susan walked downstairs. It was quiet, so she sat on the window seat in the library and read while she waited for Grayson. The library curtains were drawn, so she pulled them open. A few dust motes which had escaped the earlier cleaning shimmered in the sunshine that poured into the room, even at such an early hour. The light was perfect to read by, so she selected her well-worn copy of *Pride and Prejudice*, curled up on the gold velvet window cushion, and read the first line.

It is a truth universally acknowledged, that a single man in possession of a good fortune, must be in want of a wife.

She laughed to herself. *And likewise, it is conventionally understood that an unmarried woman should agree to being bartered as a wife to a single man of any level of fortune who knocks at their door and asks for their hand, for the women should have no feelings on the topic of marriage,* she thought cynically.

She thumbed open the first few pages, but she realized she was more interested in trying to catch the one she wanted before they forced her to marry an old curmudgeon. Grayson would be here soon. Susan closed the book and leaned back on the cushion, surveying her surroundings. Papa and Mama had spent hours in here together. He would do his accounts, Mama would read, and Susan played with her toys on the carpet. She always enjoyed spending time in this room. The dark mahogany wood of the furniture and the spacious plan provided a calmness that she craved.

The sound of rustling startled her before a small black head popped out from under Papa's desk.

"It must be warm under there, Noelle. Did I disturb your sanctuary?" Her kitty leaped from the floor to her lap, and after pawing the fabric of the skirt, she settled down to purr.

"Grayson will be here soon, so you need to stay in my room." Susan had grown protective towards Noelle, hating to leave her while Prucilla remained. Since Rose was coming with them, she could not ask her to watch over Noelle. Besides, she had mentioned none of her suspicions to Rose. With Prucilla away, however, perhaps she could just lock her bedroom door. Prucilla rarely made a practice of going into her room. Placing the kitty on her shoulder, she left the library and headed back to her bedroom. She had just reached the top of the stairs when she heard Gibbs open the door to Grayson. She waited, tucked next to the wall, out of sight, wanting to glimpse him.

"Good morning, Lord Harding. Your lordship, Lady Susan will be down shortly. Permit me to show you to the parlour, where there is a fire to warm you."

"Thank you, Gibbs.

She craned her neck and looked down into the hall. *He brought me white roses!* She ran to her room and rang the bell. Alice, the upstairs maid, came quickly.

"Alice, would you please ask Rose to join me in the parlour? Lord Harding has arrived." The young, dark-haired girl bobbed her head and hurried away.

Susan gave her sweet kitty a kiss on the head and laid her atop the pillows on the bed. Waiting a moment longer to watch the cat wriggle beneath the smaller pillow's edge, she warned:

"Stay quiet and out of sight while I am gone." Noelle's purr ran loud, as if in answer.

"Good." Susan checked herself in her mirror and grabbed her lavender pelisse from her wardrobe. As she approached the parlour, she overheard Rose and Grayson talking.

"Oh, m'lady will enjoy these beauties. I will put them in a vase of water." Rose beamed with approval.

"Thank you, Rose."

"M'lady was ready, but found she needed to make a change to her *toilette* b'fore she left. She will be down in a moment, you may be sure."

Susan walked into the room and gasped at the bouquet of white and barely pink roses in Grayson's hands.

"They are beautiful, Grayson. Thank you." She sighed, and taking the flowers, held them to her nose. "Mm... they smell delightful and are so lovely. Where did you find such beautiful roses... and such pale pink ones... the colour is so sheer it resembles a hint of a blush?"

"If you find them thus, then I have been successful, my lady, and I will endeavour to remember they are a favourite of yours." Grayson smiled and bowed.

"Mama always loved white roses, and I am partial to them as well," she gabbled, recovering quickly to add, "but the addition of these pink ones...well, I have never seen them coloured such a delicate pink. I believe they *are* my new favourite." She gazed up at him, unable to keep her eyes from his full lips and aching to know what they would feel like. It might never happen, but a girl was allowed her dreams...and she had done just *that*. She had dreamed of his kisses. A slight heat rose up her neck at the thought, and she smelled the roses once more, hoping to hide any sign of her blush from that knowing gaze.

"I am very glad you like them. I should, perhaps, mention that they came from the greenhouses at Bellmane. We have several potted ones which are moved inside before the winter so that we have them throughout the year. Are you still feeling well enough for a drive and perhaps a picnic? There is a grassy ridge that overlooks the building of the new Pavilion. Many people find it a suitable place for a picnic. I have brought along a basket of food for just such an outcome."

"That sounds lovely." *In fact, it sounds wondrous!* "I would love to go on such an outing. Do we need a blanket? I can soon have one fetched."

"There is no need, my lady. I have everything we shall require. I even have a special blanket for Rose, and another basket of food for Rose and the groom."

"How thoughtful, m'lord." Rose beamed and gave a quick bob of her head in acknowledgement.

A delightful shiver rippled through Susan's body at the thought of partaking of a picnic with Grayson. *Why am I putting myself in the way of such heartbreak? In a few weeks, I will either have to run away or marry some old reprobate. Thanks to Prucilla and Papa, Grayson is beyond my reach.*

Despite her best efforts at reason, she could not seem to stop the attachment to him, which was forming inside. It gave her a sliver of hope. *I do not plan to run away, of course, but there must be other choices. I may have to be creative in my thinking.* She smiled to herself, despite the predicament she faced.

Susan was a vision. Her lavender dress, decorated with small flowers, and the lavender pelisse and white muff, showed her off to perfection. Her blonde hair was pinned up in a simple arrangement, allowing small tendrils to frame her face. Grayson imagined he had seen her amber eyes light up when she saw him, but could not be certain he did not will her reaction. He could not help himself. Whenever he saw Susan, he smiled, especially when he considered she would soon be his wife, someone with whom he could raise a family and share his dreams. He loved her and dared to hope that one day he would win Susan's heart—and not chase her off by having arranged the betrothal papers behind her back.

He and Satterfield had signed the papers only yesterday but had decided not to discuss them for the time being, to allow him time to court Susan. Grayson had been willing to put off signing them, but the Marquess seemed eager to have it done as a protection for his children should something befall him. That Prucilla could want to rid the world of his son appeared to have unnerved Satterfield. Alex had taken to riding in the fresh air with the same fervour Grayson had noticed with Susan and her horse, Smudge.

The young lord objected to relinquishing his time with his father or his attachment to Night Star, complaining when they called an end to the day. Grayson had gifted the pony to Satterfield for Alex—that had always been his intent—but he agreed to keep the animal at Bellmane for the time being. Satterfield rather seemed to enjoy the time with his son, away from his wife's demands. Grayson suspected the man simply liked being away from her. The Marquess had told him that only the night before he had searched her room but found no sign of a bottle with arsenic powder. Afraid to let down his guard, Satterfield had said he planned to speak with Daniel more closely, as soon as he could.

Before leaving Bellmane to see Susan, Grayson had sought out father and son. He had found the Marquess watching Alex ride Night Star around the paddock on his own. Grayson had brought his barouche so they could accommodate Susan's sleepy chaperone. He chuckled when he thought of her, imagining that she would fall asleep rather quickly. The carriage offered a more comfortable ride and would make it easier to view the Pavilion. The park they were going to today would certainly be removed when the new palace was completed, as it offered too much public intrusion.

"Sir, your greatcoat. It is sunny today, but it could turn cold in a trice." Gibbs' voice broke in on his thoughts, and he realized he had been staring at Susan while smiling like a greenhorn.

"Grayson, I believe we are ready. I will arrange the roses when we return. They are exquisite."

"Thank you, Gibbs." He accepted his coat from the butler and, having escorted the ladies down the steps, helped them into the carriage.

"'Tis a lovely day, m'lord. We are most fortunate in the weather. 'opefully, the warmth will 'old." Rose leaned back, smiling, and made herself comfortable in the seat facing them. As she became more relaxed, the small bag of needle-work she had brought with her slipped to the floor. The faint hum of her soft snores filled the air. Susan reached over and gently covered her maid with a blanket.

When they arrived at the point of vantage he had proposed, his groom found a grassy area spacious enough that they could spread out a thick blanket for their picnic and observe the Pavilion and its lovely grounds. Their space was partially obscured from other visitors enjoying the area by beautiful pink and red camellia bushes and other small evergreens. Several parties lounged on blankets with their own picnic baskets, although the little knots of people were spread out enough to give them all some semblance of privacy. Grayson handed the groom the extra basket intended for Rose and the groom, and the tiger found a place nearby, yet still affording some privacy. Rose's snores had not paused, so he offered Susan his arm and they walked towards a lush grassy area just beyond the barouche.

"I hope you are hungry. I had Cook prepare cheeses, bread, fruits... and this." He held out a small carafe of red wine and two glasses. "Susan, please hold this for a moment." He offered her a glass, and removing the glass stopper from a clear crystal decanter, poured a small amount of wine.

"This is so nice, Grayson. I have not seen the Pavilion from here. When it is finished, I fear I shall never have occasion to see within, so to observe the outside is wonderful. It gives me so much ability to imagine what it will look like when it is completed. However, I do not think I can even imagine what the inside will be like, with so much Eastern influence."

"It is colourful, and far more ostentatious than is to my liking, but the Regent is known for his lavish lifestyle. It is one of comfort and influence. I understand he plans to spend a great deal of time here in Brighton, which precipitated his need for this palace." Reaching into the basket, he removed some of the cold meats and cheeses and two plates. "I hope these are to your liking, Susan."

"It looks wonderful. Thank you." She took a small selection of foods on to her plate and tasted a piece of cheese."

Her eyes sparkled as she sipped her wine and surveyed the construction of the palace, and he was moved by their beauty. Without thinking, he leaned forward and brushed her lips with his own. Susan did not move and for an instant he thought he had stepped beyond bounds. He pulled back at once, yet even as he did so, she reached up and put her hand behind his head, gently urging him closer. Grayson needed no more encouragement. He had indulged a few desires of late, including wondering how it would be to kiss her plump lips. Without further hesitation, he covered her mouth with his and coaxed her with the tip of his tongue. When she responded with hesitant touches of her own tongue, a soft moan escaped her lips, and he took advantage, seeking the warmth of her mouth. It tasted like wine.

"Grayson, Rose… Oh…"

"She has not moved an inch since we halted the carriage." Gently, he leaned her back against his arm so he could nibble her neck.

"That is undoubtedly true…but what if she should wake?"

"Worry not, my love. She is sound asleep." He covered her mouth once more, shocked when she feverishly responded, her body wantonly nudging his own in a manner he was sure she was unaware of. It was what he wanted but could not take. Not now; not like this. He momentarily felt lost and completely out of control as together they were swept away in an endless kiss.

"Umph." Susan's doubt was clear. She stretched up and gently pushed him away. "Grayson, if we are seen, we would be compromised, and I do not wish to do that to you."

He was uncertain what she meant. *Does she mean she does not want to marry me or is it that she does not want to be forced to marry...me?* He should not have signed the betrothal papers. Either way, disappointment and cold anxiety threatened to undo him.

"Perhaps we should leave." *The words came from my mouth, but they are not what my heart is saying.* "Rose has not moved, but I doubt she will bring attention to her inattention. Nevertheless, my lady, mayhap it is better we return."

"Grayson, please pardon my forwardness, but I beg you will not say you made a mistake by kissing me. I could not bear it if you were… displeased." Her face twisted with emotion.

He should be scandalized, but this was his Susan and she had never been one to toy with the truth, no matter what it had cost her as a young girl. He should not be surprised she had not changed. Grayson smiled, thinking of all the outra-geous conversations and activities they had done as children.

More than once over the years, he had recalled one escapade of hers in particular, because it had been so charac-teristic of Susan. She had wanted 'stars' in her bedchamber, and had gone about the meadows one night, capturing glow flies in a jar, all of which she had then released into her room. Susan had later told him of the captivating, fairy-like bursts of starlight piercing the dark of her room and had congratulated herself on her idea. However, she had been wholly unprepared for the revelation in the morning that the glow flies were very unattractive by day. It took her days to locate all the creatures she had released and return them to the outdoors.

He looked back at the carriage. The groom and tiger were occupied with their basket, and Rose still slept.

"How can you think me displeased? You always were a silly chit! I shall permit myself one more kiss to show you the error of your ways, my lady, and then, I fear, we must leave."

"Very good, my lord," Susan said in a contrite tone, which did not deceive him for a moment. Leaning against him, she wrapped her arms around his neck.

Her touch stirred him beyond reason, making it hard to control his body's reaction. He met her lips with his own, the warmth and movement of their tongues inciting him further as they parried and parted in the French manner, teasing and tasting as though starved. She was a banquet fit for the Prince's table and if he did not stop, he would devour her. On the thought, he broke the kiss, and in the same instant, hated himself.

CHAPTER 9

*S*usan had never been kissed, let alone been kissed so thoroughly. Her body hummed with an excitement she had not experienced before. The warmth of his tongue and his hands made her feel... loved... and wanted. She wanted more of something she could not understand, and yet knew better than to let this continue. She had to stop, but equally, had never felt so gripped by a force beyond her control.

When she had spoken of being compromised, Grayson's face had briefly grimaced with pain and something else she could not read. The fear that he would apologize for kissing her unnerved her more than the outrageous way she had reacted. She had behaved scandalously, but as always, the words had flown from her mouth before they could be suppressed by her brain. Thankfully, Grayson seemed not to have changed where she was concerned. They were friends, no matter what the fates had in store.

"Why did you stop?" she demanded, her voice breathless as she fought to hold back tears which were threatening to break.

"Forgive me, my love. I did not want to stop; you must believe that, but I had to. Had I not, and had we been discovered…" Grayson caught her hands.

"Would that have been so dreadful?" She twisted from his grip and faced him, suddenly indignant and confused, overwhelmed by a sense of betrayal she could not control. She was being contrary, and she knew it. While she had not wished to be discovered, to hear he did not want to compromise her felt different. "It is time we returned," she said stiffly, summoning all the dignity she could command. Bending down, she threw the remnants of their picnic into the basket and snatched up the blanket. She held it pointedly in his direction.

He ignored it and stood with his hands on his hips. "One moment, if you please. A matter of minutes ago, you said you were afraid of being compromised, yet when I allude to the same you become angry?"

His mouth twisted as though he were in pain, and a deep furrow appeared between his brows. His broad chest lifted in a single, mighty breath, and then he wordlessly took the proffered basket and blanket.

In silence, they walked to the carriage. As he helped her into the vehicle, Rose awoke with a start.

"Oh, m'lord. Seems I may 'ave dozed a mite." The older woman slid over in her seat and propped herself in the corner with her head bent so that her bonnet obscured her face.

Susan was already feeling remorse for her harsh words. *Forgive me* came to her lips, but she bit back the words.

"Would it have been so dreadful to have been discovered with me?" she asked as the carriage pulled forward. Within those few minutes, Rose was again softly snoring and oblivious to their conversation.

"You are wilfully misunderstanding me, Susan. I would

not wish for you to be shamed into marriage. I cannot believe such a beginning could be aught but detrimental to the communion of two minds and hearts."

I would prefer it to the way I am to be married...bartered off to some lecherous, overfed earl. She wanted to tell him of her situation but feared what he would think if he knew she had accepted his escort while being more or less promised to another. Papa had probably signed the papers. She had no way of knowing. She just knew she had no intention of going through with any betrothal to a crusty old peer of her father's choosing. If only she could think of an alternative plan...and what of her heart? Did it not matter in this?

"My lord, I thank you for the picnic. I very much enjoyed seeing the Pavilion. It will be a glorious building when completed, do you not agree? I do not think I could ever have imagined such a structure, had I not seen it for myself...and to think it is here in Brighton." Susan forced a smile; she wanted to say more but could not bring herself to do so for fear she would ramble, and he would know there was something she was not telling. She had no wish to engage in that conversation. *For goodness' sake, I am already rambling to myself!*

"I agree. The Prince Regent seems to favour the town, and it is quite an honour to have him lavish such time and money here. I can see for myself the effect it has had in the time I have been absent. There is tremendous growth, especially along the coast and with the fishermen." Grayson smiled, too, but it lacked his usual warmth. She wanted to throw something and stamp her foot. *We are talking about fish?* The stilted conversation annoyed her, even though she realized it was her fault. She had taken offence, and his explanation had soothed all but her own abrupt behaviour. Her heart urged her to find something to break the tension, but stubborn pride fought against it.

They drove in silence for what seemed like an interminable period. She could not withstand the silence any longer, especially knowing it was her bad-tempered remarks which had placed them in this situation.

"I have heard that the Prince Regent is a lover of balls?" She blurted the question without thinking first. "Do you think there will be one when the Pavilion finally opens?" she added, to minimize the stupidity of the question. *Of course, he will throw a ball.* The tension was really affecting her common sense.

Grayson quirked a brow. "Yes, I suppose he will. Are you angling for an invitation?" He flashed her a smile—one that oozed annoyance.

Of all the nerve! "No, *Lord* Harding, I was merely making polite conversation. Of course, I am not *angling* for an invitation." She crossed her arms and moved to the far corner of the seat, hoping he would get the message.

"We will be back at your father's house shortly and you will be relieved of my company, which suddenly seems to annoy you." He looked sad as he spoke, and his face suddenly appeared tired.

Apologize at once. Her mother's voice was as loud and clear as a bell. No one else in the carriage seemed to hear it. It was as if Mama were here, admonishing her for her earlier tone. Susan knew she deserved it, but she did not want to apologize. She wanted to argue—with someone, anyone—because she did not want to marry that slobbering Lord Aldrington who visited Papa. She shuddered with the thought. It had not missed her notice that he had visited *twice* this week. She should speak with Papa, but had avoided discussing the betrothal, hoping it would miraculously disappear.

"Grayson, do you know Lord Aldrington?" *Why was she asking Grayson about him?* She regretted the question immediately.

"In a manner of speaking. I have not seen him in years, but he was an acquaintance of my father's. I cannot say he was much more. If I remember correctly, Father always complained speaking with Aldrington made him feel like he was standing in the rain." He gave her a wink. "Why do you ask about Lord Aldrington?"

"No reason. He has been to visit Papa twice lately. It just seems peculiar, that is all." She knew he would not settle for that reason, but it was all she wanted to say. She should not have mentioned his name. What had possessed her to do that?

"Has he displeased you, Lady Susan?"

"No, Grayson, he has not. It was just an odd thought. I was trying to make conversation and my thoughts were rambling, I am afraid."

"I see." Grayson turned away.

Apologize! Mama's voice seemed louder this time. Susan looked around, but she was the only one who seemed to have heard it.

"Please forgive me, Grayson…" She did not dare say more and hoped he would not ask—Susan was not sure she could make a better apology. She hated being wrong.

He nodded, and his face at once relaxed its severity. "I forgive you. If I upset you, I would be happy to apologize."

"No. It is merely my testiness. My nerves are disordered these days."

"With your brother so ill, it is understandable."

"Yes. I am glad you appreciate all that is happening… and that is why I cannot abide this hostility between us, Grayson. I hope you will forgive my temper."

"If you are sure that is all there is to the matter." He lifted the corners of his mouth into a smile. "My love, you have nothing for which to apologize. I should have chosen my words more carefully."

He called me his love. He called me his love! Her heart thrummed with hope.

"M'lady, you surely 'aven't said something peevish to his lordship?" Her sleepy maid opened blue-grey eyes, which at once, seemed focused on her.

Why, Rose was a sly one; she had been listening! "Of course not, Rose," she said, in a tone calculated to squash any further such pretensions, but her suddenly lighter mood would not allow her to be angry with the maid. *He called me his love.* Could it be foolish fancy that he truly had feelings for her, beyond those of friendship?

As if in answer to her silent question, Grayson reached over and gently picked up her gloved hand and held it to his lips.

"My lady, Susan, would you be amenable to riding with me later this week—perhaps tomorrow, if the weather holds?"

Susan looked around. They were turning onto Hovis Road, the road which connected their properties, so she would be home shortly.

"Yes. Yes, I believe I would like that."

"Splendid. I shall look forward to it. I have something very important to tell you, but it will wait until tomorrow."

"Not now?" What could it be about this that made her nervous?

"No, not now, Miss Curiosity. It will wait." He leaned over and kissed her on the nose.

She noticed Rose's eyes directed at the two of them, but even the scrutiny of an imperious maid could not dampen the rush of joy which flooded her being.

Gibbs opened the door almost before they reached the top step. The man bowed, his stooping frame curving towards his knees as he did so. "My lord, welcome. My lady, your father asked me to inform you that Lord Alexander is accompanying him."

"Where is Papa?"

"He was called away to meet with his man of business. He left about two hours ago but indicated he would return shortly." Gibbs stepped away to hang the coats on the stand, but then turned back to her. "You should know the Marchioness has been asking for you." His eyelid flickered by the tiniest degree. In a lesser individual, Susan would have considered him guilty of winking, but Gibbs? Surely not!

That the odious woman was looking for her irritated Susan beyond measure, but she held her tongue on that particular topic, charmed by this evidence of the old retainer's support.

"Gibbs, was she with Alex before Papa left?" She had to know, now extremely worried about her brother's safety.

"No, my lady. She has not, to my knowledge."

Susan waited for Rose to leave the entrance hall before looking up at Grayson.

"Thank you again for a delightful day, my lord." Susan's voice was laden with emotion.

"It was nothing, Lady Susan. Your company was its own reward." He smiled, a polite smile from one friend to another. "I am sure we will meet again ere long, now I am returned home."

The words were no more than a polite leave-taking. Yet when Grayson lifted her gloved hand and kissed it, a pleasing warmth coursed through her and, most shockingly, delivered a strange, tickling sensation to the centre of her abdomen. "I must leave now," he continued, "but I will call again, if you are amenable to my visits."

Guilt assailed Susan at her duplicity, but she held firm in her resolve not to spoil this time with Grayson. With one eye on Gibbs' impassive countenance, she replied:

"What a shrew you must think me! Of course, I am amenable to your visits. You are such an old and dear friend. Seeing you again, it is almost as though you did not leave. I cannot imagine this Christmastide without your presence, now that you have returned home." Unless, of course, she thought dourly, she was dragged to the altar in the meantime. Strangely, however, the hours spent with Grayson gave her hope.

"Until the next time, then." Lifting his hat, he bowed and left. She stared after him for several minutes, following his carriage's departure from her view.

The tapping of her stepmother's footsteps disturbed her concentration.

"There you are, my dear. I have been looking for you. Was that Lord Harding with you?" She did not wait for an answer. "We have guests coming for tea. I would like for you to meet them."

Susan inclined her head politely, little though she wished to. "*Who* is coming, Stepmother?" Biting back the bile that threatened, she tried to sound interested. She had no desire to spend any of her time with Prucilla. All she wanted to do was retire to her chamber to think about this morning and Grayson…and when she could meet with him again.

"I met Lady Jacobson in town today. She was with her sister, Lady Harvey. I have invited them to make a short visit since they have only just come to Brighton, and I have not seen Marie Jacobson in an age! They should be here soon. We moved in the same circles, you know. Marie and I came out together, but alas, the poor girl was not able to achieve the match she angled after."

Susan watched her stepmother's face as she spoke, and she could have sworn Prucilla's lips curled in a sneer as she mentioned Lady Jacobson's name. Why, then, was she inviting her to ruin a perfectly good day? *What is she about now?*

Susan followed Prucilla from the entrance hall, but quickly made her excuses and scurried off to her room, determined to have some time alone before the ladies arrived. She needed to think...and ensure that Noelle was safe. Her room should still be locked. It was.

<hr/>

G rayson heard Lady Satterfield coming their way and chose to depart. The less he saw of that woman, the better, he reasoned. He spent some time with his horses in the stables, listening to news of Night Star's progress from Jason, his head groom. Satterfield and Alex had been there that very morning. On arrival at the house, it surprised him to find the Duke of Hollingbury's carriage in the forecourt.

"Rudolph, thank you." He stood while Rudolph removed his greatcoat. "I see His Grace is here?"

"Yes, my lord. He arrived a short while ago and insisted they needed to wait for your return. I have put them in your study." The butler's voice bellowed in the small entrance hall.

"They?" Grayson echoed.

"Yes, my lord. A Mr. Michaelmas..." He coughed loudly. "... is with His Grace. He gave me to understand he is an investigator." The servant's disapproval was apparent in his voice.

"Thank you, Rudolph. I will attend to them." Grayson

appreciated his butler, but sometimes, like today, the older man's loud voice betrayed his personal feelings. As irritating and embarrassing as it could be, it still made him smile—and of a certainty it could make things interesting with his guests.

Grayson chuckled as he opened the door to his study, ready to welcome Cooper, but the expression on his friend's face stopped him.

"Cooper, why the black look?"

"Come, sit down. We have news."

"Yes, please." He walked to his desk and perched on the corner.

"This is Alan Michaelmas, the best Bow Street Runner I have known. He has news and has also heard rumours. I think it would be prudent to hear both, as they could be important."

"You have my full attention." Grayson felt his chest clench as he sensed the news was worse than previously imagined.

"She was in town again today, my lord." The Runner faced Grayson. "She left her carriage at the milliner's and waited for it to leave. I followed the Marchioness to the apothecary's shop, two streets away. Her maid did not leave the millinery shop. When Lady Satterfield left the apothecary's shop, we questioned the druggist. She is not his favourite customer, and he was happy to repeat all that she said. She has been in several times over the past dozen weeks or more. Small bottles, that is all she requests. Her ladyship does not offer explanations, and the apothecary is not in the habit of asking for one. She did mutter something about a pregnancy and a child not being second. Today she also purchased laudanum."

"Dear God! Does she plan to combine them?" Grayson knew the answer, but was shocked. He knew the combination of the two could be lethal, with laudanum covering for the effects of the arsenic.

"Everything we assumed about her actions may be true, Gray. We need to find the Marquess."

"His lordship and young Alex have visited several times over the past few days. The young lord is looking much better. I believe the fresh air has been good for him. That and less porridge. We believe Lady Satterfield has been using that as her conduit for the poison."

"I escorted Susan home before returning here. Lord Satterfield had not returned when I left. I fear for both Susan and her brother, if what you are saying is true. I wish we had some proof to offer the Marquess."

"We have. I believe she must have left this behind today, by accident." He held up a white lace handkerchief with the Marchioness' initials in the corner. "Lady Satterfield dropped it on the floor by the counter and must not have missed it."

"I must go back to the Winslow estate." Realization of what could happen unnerved Grayson. He pulled the bell and the butler appeared. "Rudolph, have my horse brought around and send a groom for Dr. Steth and ask him to meet us at the Satterfield Hall."

"Yes, sir," the butler thundered, his face wearing a look of confusion. Grayson grabbed his greatcoat from the boot room and the moment a panting groom came running up with Blacklock, the three men set off toward the Winslow estate.

Susan praised her lucky stars when she found Noelle well, and alone in her room. She briefly wondered how long Prucilla had been home and what she had been doing, but it was fleeting. The moment she picked up Noelle and heard her purr, she forgot everything else.

"Noelle, I have missed you. I will ring for some milk. You seem rested, but I am sure you are hungry." Reaching the bell-rope in a few steps, she pulled it, and, within minutes, Rose appeared.

"There you be, m'lady. We had barely stepped inside, and you disappeared. Your stepmother seemed rather displeased by something when I walked past the parlour, having put off my coat and hat. Then your father arrived, and she went to her room." The maid set down a tray, on which reposed a cup of steaming liquid. "I thought you might like some chocolate and went to the kitchen, but Cook seems to have had the same notion. I found this sitting on the table, waiting fer you. It is nice and warm; 'twill be just the thing to settle you."

"Thank you, Rose." She sipped the beverage and sighed. "I love chocolate." Susan swallowed some more of the warm liquid before setting the cup down again. "I had a delightful time this morning, Rose."

"Yes, m'lady. You and Lord Harding have always been firm friends. If your dear mother were still here, she would have been as pleased as puddin' to see the two of you recover the thread of your childhood affection."

Noelle sauntered over and sniffed the cup. "Shoo, Noelle. That is for me." Susan picked up the warm cup and took another drink. "This is good and most welcome. Thank you, Rose, and be sure to thank Cook."

"I will do that." The old woman smiled and nodded.

"Stepmother wishes me to help her entertain some ladies this afternoon," Susan remarked. "It seems they were present at her own coming out." Suddenly, she felt light-headed. Rising, she walked to the window, hoping the movement would make her feel better. "She dares to mention that when she will not allow me one of my own!"

"Now, m'lady, no good ever comes of crying over spilt milk. You must trust your papa to do right by you. Don't let her upset you so. Your dear mama would say as 'tis the mark of a lady to ignore the strutting of ill-mannered widgeons."

"Rose! I am quite sure Mama—" Susan broke off and watched the maid clear a shawl, a pair of gloves, and a book from a chair. Did she intend to stay and talk? *Please... no. I want to think.* From the corner of her eye, Susan saw Noelle paw the cup of chocolate she had left on the table near her bed. Before she could reach it, the cat slapped it again, knocking it over and spilling its contents onto the floor. The warm, dark liquid soaked into the carpet almost immediately.

"Oh, wicked kitty! Noelle! What a dreadful mess." She rushed over, realizing she had nothing she could use to clean it. "Why did you do such a thing?"

"Bah! You are a naughty, ungrateful little cat. What use have you for chocolate, pray? Fish-heads, that's what you should have!" Rose declared.

"Meeeooooow!" Noelle washed her paws and then, undaunted by these strictures, left the empty cup and scampered back to the soft pillows on Susan's bed.

Rose shooed Susan away from the mess. "M'lady, you will soil your gown. I will see to that. I have never seen her do such a thing before." She shook her head in disbelief. "Why not rest on your bed for a while? I will soon have the room ship-shape, again."

"I think I will. I feel rather… unsteady." She sat down on the edge of her bed. Her voice sounded a little thick, even to her own ears. "I am not sure what it might be, but Prucilla is engaged in some madness; I cannot shake the feeling. Poor Grayson, I think he knew she was coming and he all but dashed away after he set us down."

Susan was tired, yet she did not want to sleep. She wanted to think about Grayson and how to escape from here without getting married. And she also wanted her portmanteau packed—in case matters progressed beyond her capabilities, and a need arose to escape quickly. She could not let Rose know, so she would have to do that on her own. *I should do that before I lie down, but I do not have the energy to get up.* Where would she go? While Susan had relatives, she was uncertain she felt confident enough to ask for their help.

I must think about this, but I feel so tired. She wished she might marry Grayson. *A miracle would be easier! Although, indeed, it is the season for that,* she thought wryly. Maybe she should pray for that…she had always wanted a Christmastide wedding. It was her favourite time of year. Now, she realized she was unlikely to see the wedding of her dreams, much less one during this season. At least she had that kiss to hold on to—and she planned to keep those memories tucked safely alongside her dreams.

"There you are, young lady! You did not come downstairs and visit with my guests. They are gone now. I hope you know how much you embarrassed me." Prucilla's shrill voice pierced her ears. *Goodness gracious!* Susan opened her eyes, not realizing she had closed them, and looked up at her stepmother. The woman was holding a cup towards Susan and sneering in a sinister fashion.

"I have brought you some tea, little though you deserve such attention."

Susan started to say something—she knew not what—but Noelle leaped from behind her and, knocking the cup of hot tea from Prucilla's hand, landed upon her stepmother. Scaling the woman's arm, Noelle clambered up to Prucilla's elaborate coiffure and planted her four legs in its depths. Prucilla shrieked in terror and tried desperately, at one and the same time, to pull the cat off and run away. It was the most extraordinary sight. Prucilla was running in circles around the room.

"MEOW." Noelle gave a last dig with her claws, leaped to

the floor and ran off between Prucilla's legs, disappearing down the hall through the open door.

"Whatever is all the noise? I heard the screaming from downstairs. What in the world is this madness?" The Marquess rushed into the room, frantic, gasping and red-faced from the run up the stairs.

"Papa... I am sure I cannot tell you. Prucilla brought me tea and Noelle launched herself at the cup." Susan could barely keep her eyes open. She had to get up and find her cat before Prucilla did.

A moment later, Grayson and two other men thundered into the room. Susan glimpsed Daniel and Gibbs waiting in the hall. Rose came in, holding a pile of towels and a pail; she dropped the towels at the sight in front of her.

"What is going on here? Duke Hollingbury, Lord Harding —what do you think you are about, to be entering my daughter's bedchamber?" the Marquess yelled.

"Stop her!" Grayson pointed to the Marchioness. "Lord Satterfield, we have proof that your wife could be responsible for your son's condition."

"That is an outrageous accusation. Husband, you do not believe such fiddle-faddle, surely?" Prucilla looked about to have an apoplexy; her eyes were starting from her head and a vein pulsed on her brow. "Her cat attacked me and now I am forced to listen to such vile accusations?" She turned to the footman. "Daniel, I demand you find that cat. I will take care of it." She then tried to leave the room, but Daniel and another man Susan did not recognize blocked her exit. Susan felt herself sway...

"How dare you! I am a marchioness. Out of my way." Prucilla tried to force her way from the room.

"You will sit, Wife!" Susan heard Papa's voice boom in a tone and level she had never heard before. "I will hear what they have to say." He turned to Grayson. "Harding, you have accused my wife of a villainous crime. You had better have proof."

"I do, your lordship." He produced a handkerchief with her initials. "My lady, I believe you left this at the apothecary this morning."

"Did you visit the apothecary this morning, Lady Satterfield?"

"Y... yes, I did... but to get something for... oh, dear, now you are putting me to the blush, dearest." Recovering her temper, she smiled sweetly. Susan wondered if anyone else noticed how false it was. "I did so want this joyous news to be something we shared..."

"Are you trying to tell me you are with child?"

"Yes. I have had bouts of nausea in the mornings and sought a remedy to give me some ease. Unfortunately, the chemist could not furnish me with what I needed."

"That *would* be a blessed event, indeed," her father bit out slowly.

As bad as Susan felt at this minute, laughter threatened, forcing her to look away to avoid chuckling at the woman's embarrassment. Her father would not share her amusement.

"I do not believe you, wife, but I will give you the benefit of the doubt. I will have you examined by Dr. Steth. If you are *enceinte*, he will confirm it." The Marquess spoke the words in a cold, harsh voice.

"How dare you speak to me thus, sir? You question my word about such a joyous event, and in front of these persons? I tell you now, I will choose my physician. How dare you!"

"Why were you really there, Prucilla? And for what purpose did you come to Susan's bedchamber?" Satterfield looked behind him and nodded towards her maid. "Rose, please search her ladyship's person."

Rose walked across the room to search the Marchioness'

reticule and any pockets in her gown and robe, before also feeling along the seams of her clothing.

Prucilla slapped Rose's hands as the maid extracted, from a hidden pocket in the former's dress, a small blue-green bottle filled with liquid. Rose held the object in a firm grip and passed it to Lord Satterfield. With the assembled's attention on this shocking discovery, the Marchioness tried to flee, but Daniel and the other man filled the doorway and blocked her exit from the room.

Susan lost her ability to sit upright any longer. She tried to lift her head, but its weight was too much, and she swayed again, this time with more violence, until she fell backwards onto the mattress. She heard Noelle's loud purring in her ear and Grayson's voice calling her name. His voice was getting further and further away. Her head was spinning, and little was making sense. She hoped sleep would provide sweet dreams, Prucilla would forget to have her summoned for tea, and Rose would leave her in peace for a while. Her eyes drifted closed, and soon all she could hear was Noelle's purr echoing in her head.

 *week later*

Susan fought against waking up from this dream. It was a different life, one that elicited constant smiles and kisses. She was engaged to marry Grayson, and they were racing Smudge and Blacklock neck and neck across the meadows behind his stables. Lavender and wild poppies carpeted the hooves of the animals as they cleared low wooden fences and small streams. Laughter filled the air. She was gloriously happy... there was only light, love and...

"M'lady, you must get up!" Rose pulled back the covers. "I 'ate to do this to you, my love, but you have a caller. He 'as been waiting, but the posies he brought you are wilting." There was no admonishment in her maid's voice. "And yer cat is being called to come too." She huffed in mock affront. "In all me years, I 'ave never 'ad a cat receive a caller!"

Susan lay still, hoping she could return to the meadow, her horse and Grayson... but it was winter, not spring, and there were no flowers carpeting the meadow. Reality was as cold as a mackerel on a fishmonger's slab. There had been no ride across Bellmane, and except for friendship, there was no Grayson. She pulled the pillow over her head, a last attempt to regain the quiet she had been enjoying moments before.

Noelle's purring stopped abruptly, and her tail began swishing back and forth and up and down, hitting her pillow. In cat language, Susan imagined these movements meant, 'go away.'

"Come along, Noelle. We have company." She tossed the pillow back and swung her legs over the side of her bed, relishing the warmth of the carpet and the room. A housemaid made sure that her fireplace was always lit well before the day broke.

She was not anxious to go downstairs and meet the fubsy old earl who planned to marry her. She had pushed Papa as far as she knew it to be reasonable, and today, she must decide… stay and marry or leave. This was the deal her father and Prucilla had arranged for her, and she hated it more than ever.

"Rose… Prucilla will not be…?" Dread now filled her every time she thought of the woman.

"No, m'lady. They took her away, they did. She cannot 'urt you or your brother." The maid looked heavenward and then crossed herself. "A most unfortunate thing. When I think about what she tried to do, it sends shivers through me whole body."

"I still cannot believe she wanted to poison us. She is a spiteful, wicked woman." The thought of how close she might have been to dying forced a shiver. "Who is the caller, Rose?" She needed to change the subject. Walking to the fireplace, she held her hands out to warm them. It was habit more than anything else. The truth was, Susan did not want to hear the caller's name. She knew whoever had come was to be her betrothed, but distancing herself made it feel less real. Neither did she wish to hear more about that abhorrent woman. When she thought about what Prucilla had almost done... all because she had presumed herself with child and had wanted to remove Alex from competition with her own offspring. "Thank goodness Dr. Steth confirmed she was not with child." A chill passed over Susan. "Did you know Prucilla once had a child?"

The old woman bristled. "I know I should 'ave more respect, but that woman 'as no business being anyone's mother." Her maid looked at her, her lips pursed tightly.

"I hate to be cruel, but I agree, Rose." Would she have killed it? *Did she kill it?* A shudder shook her to the core. The truth might never be known.

"The caller, Rose? Are you going to tell me who it is?"

"Now, m'lady, I cannot tell you, so please do not ask me. I gave me oath to keep it to me self."

"You cannot tell me the name of a caller? How *odd*. Should I infer from this the gentleman is my intended? Am I not to know his identity until the day I marry him?" She pulled an unladylike face; the toothless old goat must feel pretty sure of himself—and her compliance.

"My lips are closed, m'lady. I have laid out your peach silk with the blonde lace overdress. There is a hot bath for you behind the screen.

"Thank you, Rose." Susan dropped her chemise and stepped into the tub, easing her way into its warm waters.

The greying woman nodded and smiled. "Don't be taking too long. We must hurry. I will sit on this chair and wait."

Within minutes, a soft snore rent the air, drawing Susan's attention. "Rose..." She caught herself. A few extra minutes in the jasmine scented bath could hurt no one. She slid down and relaxed, allowing the water to ease her cares.

Where is she? Does she already suspect and has decided to avoid me completely in a fit of pique? Grayson had already paced across the rug in the parlour so many times he was certain he knew the pattern count to the light gold Aubusson carpet.

"My lord?" Gibbs knocked on the door and entered. "His lordship wishes to see you in his study." He bowed and waited.

"That is an improvement over wearing out his beautiful carpet. Gibbs, would you have someone put these roses in a vase? I fear I have nearly wrung the life out of them. Perhaps water will salvage some of their beauty." He handed the flowers to the servant.

Gibbs coughed, the sound exaggerated. "Ah, yes, my lord. They do look somewhat...tormented." He took the blooms and turned to leave. Grayson thought the old man's eyes lit up with a mirth he had not seen in years.

The door to the library opened before he could knock. "Come in...come in, Harding. I fear she will take her time. My daughter has still not asked about the betrothal and it is my worry she may come down in some distress, still expecting the worst. I have kept my promise not to say anything, but I do not think I have helped your cause by doing so."

Grayson took a seat in front of Satterfield's desk and gave a small tug to his Waterfall knot—enough to barely loosen it. Despite the cold weather, he was perspiring. While a fire warmed the library, it was insufficient to cause his reaction; undoubtedly he was afflicted with nerves. It was unlike him to be nervous, but he had gone about this matter the wrong way and now had to right it, and hopefully not lose the one person whose sheer presence made him feel he was home.

Warm, happy, and home. He was no longer sure it would be as simple as that. Grayson felt in his pocket and touched the license. He *was* nervous.

"Now, my boy, you are as fidgety as a cat on hot bricks." The Marquess paused, rubbing his chin thoughtfully. "Perhaps I should not use that analogy, since the cat may have saved my daughter's life." His momentary jovial mood turned sombre.

Despite the seriousness of the Marquess' statement, Grayson chuckled. He could not help himself. Perhaps it was the tension.

"Forgive me, sir. It is nervousness, I think. I cannot remember when I have been this anxious.

"She is making you wait. I know my daughter. Take heart, however; 'tis not *you* she is making wait. 'Tis the one to whom she believes she is *betrothed*. I would stake my title on it." He cast a knowing glance at Grayson, and the two of them laughed.

Careful, Grayson. Too loud and it could be the worse for you if she thinks she is the butt of a joke. He ventured onto the subject he and his prospective father-in-law preferred to avoid. "I hate to ask this, but I know your wife's situation weighs heavily. I wondered what you have decided."

The Marquess grew quiet, his manner reflective before speaking. "I do not know the right thing to do. She is a dangerous woman, and it seems she has committed vicious and evil acts. I could not keep her here, and no longer want to be married to someone who could harm my child, or someone else. As hard as it will be, I must speak to Prinny on the question. He is due to arrive tomorrow and will doubtless influence the decision made upon her fate. I realize it could be harsh, yet I plan to ask for mercy. My hope is they will transport her to the penal colony, taking her as far away from my family as possible."

"Since she is a member of the peerage, that would be the probable outcome. Would you be amenable to Cooper... Hollingbury, rather, joining you at that interview? Not only do Prinny and Hollingbury have a unique relationship, Cooper's father was also friends with Viscount Evans, her former husband." He tapped his fingers on the desk, still preoccupied with thoughts of Susan.

"I would not mind if he were present. It might make dealing with Prucilla easier. I am so angry with myself for being taken in by that woman. She tried to discredit Anna all those years ago, and I still gave her grace and let her into my family. She convinced me she would be a wonderful mother to Alex." He leaned on his desk and rested his head in his hands. "The Bow Street Runner took her to Newgate, where she is now awaiting trial."

"Papa?" Satterfield lifted his head, and both men turned towards the door. "*Grayson?*" Susan stood in the doorway, a look of surprise on her face.

"Daughter, you have taken your time. It seems the time was well spent for you look lovely—just like your mama." The Marquess' sober expression slowly turned into a warm smile of affection. "You have a visitor, my dear," he went on. "Will you excuse me for a few minutes, Harding?"

Grayson acknowledged him with a polite nod, and the Marquess stepped from the room. As Satterfield pulled the door behind him, Grayson noticed a small black ball of fur on four legs as it darted into the room, squeezing through the gap just before the door closed. Noelle quietly took up residence on the corner of Satterfield's desk and began washing her paws.

"Grayson, I will admit I am quite surprised to see you here this morning. Had I known the caller was you..."

"Perhaps you would have hurried?" Grayson supplied with a grin, finishing her sentence.

"Well... yes." Her face coloured, and she had the grace to look abashed.

"I have something important to ask you. Perhaps the window-seat, with the light, would be a pleasant place?" He gently ushered her to the window; two feet away, she stopped and pulled back from him.

"No. I meant I was surprised to see you here. I had expected... someone else." She turned her face from him.

"Yes. Your father suspected as much." He wondered how much to say—too much and he would have a termagant on his hands. This could become awkward. Taking a deep breath, he walked past her to the window and stood there, looking out. He noticed the intricate arrangement of her mother's rosebushes, pruned and waiting for their bounty to show. *I have several colours of roses in my orangery. I should ensure we have plenty of white ones there, as well.* He could smell her fragrance of jasmine from where he stood. "I took part in something I thought to be a perfect, wonderful surprise—but realized afterwards that what I had done could be seen as thoughtless... inconsiderate, even..."

"I beg your pardon? Grayson, I have never known you to be a reckless person."

Grayson turned and walked back to Susan. She was looking at him as if he were a monster and had suddenly grown a second head. Chuckling, he reached into his pocket and pulled out a small box wrapped with green paper, emerald ribbons, and tiny silver bells.

"For *me?*" Her voice quivered.

He nodded, infusing his expression with as much earnest feeling as he could.

"For you."

"It is not yet Christmas, yet you give me a gift?" Susan searched his face, but soon stopped her questions in favour of undoing the wrappings. "Oh, Grayson! I love silver bells.

At Yuletide, Mother used to decorate with silver bells, holly, and mistletoe." She spoke nervously as she unwrapped the box.

"I recall that. Your home was always warm and festive. I loved spending time here during Christmastide." He watched her hands tremble as she opened the small package, exposing a small silver ring surmounted by a large ruby and flanked by smaller diamonds.

"I have had this in my possession for a while." His voice cracked with emotion. He picked up the ring, and holding her left hand, he gently fitted it to her fourth finger.

"B… but, I am to be…" Tears welled up in her beautiful, already luminous amber eyes.

Grayson dropped to one knee and gingerly held her left hand in both of his.

"Lady Susan Winslow, will you do me the great honour of becoming my wife? These past years away from you have forced me to take stock of what I wanted in life. More than anything else, I realized I missed you, Susan. I love you. When I am with you, no matter where I am, I know a glorious sense of being home. Please say…"

"Yes! Yes, I will marry you, Grayson." Her entire frame bobbed with glee as she completed his thought.

He rose, and she wound her arms around his neck, pulling him close. Their lips met, softly and then more urgently, until at length he edged them apart.

"Why did you stop kissing me, Grayson? Did I do something wrong?" She stepped away from him, her hurt clear in the sideways tilt to her chin.

"I have more to tell you." He hated the necessity, especially at this moment, but could risk no one saying something before he had explained.

"I am your betrothed."

"Yes, I know you are my betrothed, silly. Did you not just

ask me to…?" Realization must have hit her then, because she stopped talking.

For some seconds, she stared at him.

"You? You are my *intended?*" She looked stricken. He could see she felt betrayed and happy at the same time. Nor could she fathom how this had happened. Myriad emotions were crossing her face, one after the other. Some of them he could not recognize.

Then, without warning, she burst out laughing.

"Yes." He bit his own bottom lip, trying not to laugh, too. "I had thought to tell you, but then I decided I had badly erred. You might not feel the same way as I… and so I courted you, to give you the choice…"

"All this time, I have thought I was to marry an earl whom I pictured as being older than Beelzebub, with barely a tooth in his mouth. Do you know, I finally even considered such a marriage?" She laughed until tears ran from the corners of her eyes. "You fiend, I should be most dreadfully angry with you, but I cannot be cross when you have given me such a wonderful gift." She wiped at her tears.

"The ring is pretty, I grant you, but merely a trifle, my dear."

"*Booby!*" she murmured with warm exasperation. "The gift of your heart, I meant."

He rubbed his nose with a sheepish air and gave her a wry grin. "You are truly not angry? Dearest, I realized too late that I had not set about this business of marriage in the right way."

"No, you did not." Her tone was stern. She tempered it by curving one palm around his cheek. "How can I be outraged with the man who continually rescues me from my ill-conceived plans? I was actually considering marrying the toothless earl to save my brother from Prucilla." She slipped her arms around his neck and drew him closer to her again.

Noelle gave a soft meow from nearby and began washing her paws.

"I believe she approves of you." Susan laughed.

"Yes, she is quite a protector of yours. Thank goodness she approves. She redesigned Prucilla's hair and head! It is my understanding the woman had to be treated for the scratches."

"She deserved it."

"What she tried to do to you still scares me to the soul, my love." Grayson gazed at her beautiful, full lips so intently, he found he could no longer hold himself back. He brushed her mouth gently, teasingly.

"Love me, Grayson."

"I do, Susan. I do."

He kissed her more urgently. She fired his blood as no other before her. Drawing back a little, he nibbled the skin of her neck. Gradually, he moved lower and caressed her décolletage with small strokes, at the same time tugging her frivolous sleeve slightly until he released a full breast. He circled the areola with his tongue, lapping at it like a cat before finally taking the warm tip of her breast into his mouth.

His hands grazed her arms and then cupped her bottom. His touch sent warm ripples straight to her abdomen. She could feel the warm, moist reaction deep down inside. Was that why…? Struggling to catch her breath, she hugged him more closely. Her hands lay across the back of his neck; she tugged him closer to her, unsure of what to do, only knowing she needed him closer.

Susan arched her body towards him, her breath now coming in small pants. Sitting her against the corner of the desk, Grayson lifted her dress and felt beneath until he found that hidden part of her. His hand moved intimately over the moist centre, causing her to suck in a sharp breath. Whatever was he...? She swallowed a scream, her hand moving, unbidden, to the waistband of his breeches. Her body seemed to know where this was all leading. Perhaps she should let it guide her.

"Grayson. What are you doing?" She had never felt anything which could be so delicious and wicked at the same time.

"Loving you, my dearest. Do you wish for me to stop?"

"Yes...no. Please do not stop." She did not want this feeling to end. Her hands drifted to the fall of his breeches. Feeling incredibly wanton, she asked, "May I touch you?"

"You may, my love, but it might not be wise. I find myself starving to feel your body and claim it as my own."

She stilled her hand. She did not want to do anything which could stop the wondrous sensations rippling through her.

He stopped kissing her breast for a moment and gazed into her eyes.

Leaning forward, he caressed her face with tender kisses, and then joined his mouth with hers, possessively and passionately.

Breathless, she whispered against his lips. "Grayson, we must stop! Someone could come in and see us."

"Yes. You are right, of course, we should stop." Although he said the words, he continued to kiss her and only slowly lowered her dress.

Susan broke their kiss. Panting, she said, "Grayson, my papa could return at any moment."

He brushed a kiss across her nose and helped her straighten her gown.

"Indeed, my love, this is not the place for such activity."

Breathing heavily, he reached into the pocket of his waistcoat and pulled out a folded document.

"You have a marriage licence?" She could not resist wrapping her arms around him.

"Yes… my family knows Archbishop Nicholas, and I paid him a visit." Grayson nudged her with a small kiss and whispered into her ear. "When do you wish to marry this repugnant, toothless earl?"

She swatted him. "Oh, you rogue!" With an unladylike snort, she dissolved into giggles.

"You snorted! *Again!*" He gave his rich melodic laugh. "Would you care to be married during the Yule festivities, my dearest?"

"I have always dreamed of a Christmastide wedding. Mother and I would sit together and draw small sketches of dresses. Wait!" She walked over to a shelf and pulled down her worn copy of 'Pride and Prejudice', extracting a small paper from the back of the book and handing it to him. "My dress. I should hold it from you as a surprise. Mother and I created this together shortly before she died. To wear this dress will make it feel as though she were here to see me wed."

"I will wait to see it, then." He tilted her face up with his finger for another kiss.

A knock sounded on the door, and her father and brother entered. "Well, do we have anything to discuss?"

"Papa! You should be ashamed, allowing me to think you betrothed me to a stout, widowed old reprobate."

"Daughter, you did not give me a chance to tell you before you rushed from the room." He guffawed.

"Susan, you are going to marry Lord Harding! Papa told me. I get a new brother." Alex hopped on one foot.

"I took the liberty of sending for the modiste. She should be here soon. I thought you might need a new dress for the

Christmastide festivities. While the celebration ball is tomorrow evening and short notice, she has assured me it is possible so long as the design is not too complicated." Her father beamed at Susan, clearly pleased.

"Lord Satterfield, my mother is involved in that celebration. I should like to speak to her and find out if there could be a means that we might celebrate both our wedding and the beginning of the Christmastide festivities."

"Do you think it would be possible at this late hour?"

"Have you *met* my mother?" Grayson grinned. "If there is a way to accomplish this, she is the one to ask." He turned to Susan. "It seems we have a busy day ahead, but wonderful days lie beyond, my dear. I shall take my leave of you now and be on my way to town to see my mother." He brushed a kiss on her forehead and politely nodded to both Alex and his prospective father-in-law, and then made his way to the front door.

Susan followed him to the entrance and watched him leave. Then, stepping outside, she whirled around, clutching the small piece of paper to her heart and looking up at the sky. *This is your time, my dearest Susan.* She recognized her mother's voice, and it gave her joy and fulfilment. "Thank you, Mama," she breathed.

wo days later

Grayson's carriage rolled to the front of Satterfield Hall. The Harding party had driven to the ball together. Mother had insisted that she and Blaine stay at Bellmane and leave for the ball with him. She had arranged everything. Archbishop Nicholas would arrive an hour before the scheduled end of the evening. Alton had been pressed into service as well and had made many trips back and forth to Steinbright Manor, this year's location for the Christmastide ball. Lady Steinbright was a fellow conspirator of his mother's, so the town was surely in for a beautiful and immaculately planned event.

A small altar and cross from Bellmane's chapel had been delivered. They would take their vows among friends, but still within the confines of the church. It had been Mother's masterful idea. She and Lady Steinbright had been most excited with the notion. A selection of Susan's and her mother's favourite songs had been given to the orchestra, with precise instructions on when to play them. His mother loved planning events, and a glance across at the contented look on her face told him she had outdone herself.

Grayson checked his pocket for the gift he had bought for his beloved. A small silver bell garnished the outside of the tiny red velvet bag which held a silver ruby and diamond bracelet. With Alton's help, he had taken special pains with his dress this evening. A ruby and diamond pin enhanced his crisp, white shirt, and his perfectly tied white neckcloth. His black evening knee breeches and coat perfectly displayed his green and gold satin waistcoat. He reached into his pocket and pulled out his father's watch, flicking it open to read the time.

"I should not be long, Mother. I would like to escort Susan to her carriage."

"Certainly, my son. Please give her my warmest wishes and tell her Ambrose and I are all agog to see her at the ball. I have heard her dress is gorgeous."

Grayson nodded and got out. Smiling, he ran up the steps to the portico. He heard the Satterfield carriage pull up and watched as it halted behind his own carriage, ready for the occupants.

Gibbs opened the door and took his greatcoat. "They are ready, my lord." Grayson passed the butler his hat and, at the very same moment, saw a vision begin to descend the stairs.

Susan was dressed in pale gold satin with a red ribbon about her waist and sparkling red and white crystals adorning the edges. Her hair was pulled up into an elaborate arrangement, with loose curls framing her face and diamonds strategically placed throughout her hair. About her neck hung her mother's pearl and diamond necklace. She was magnificent.

"You look beautiful." He struggled to say more, but no other words would come forth.

"She is lovely." A beaming Lord Satterfield descended the stairs with young Lord Alex.

"I am being allowed to go to this ball, Lord Harding." The days of sunshine and exercise, and distance from his step-mother, had helped immensely. His eyes were bright, his skin clear and his blond, curly hair looked shiny, instead of the dull mien he had worn when he was so ill. Grayson could have sworn the young man had gained a couple of pounds. That was a healthy sign. He might never fully shake all the effects of the arsenic, as they had no way to know how much he had been given, but Dr. Steth was pleased with his remarkable recovery.

"Before we leave, Susan, I have a small gift for you."

"Grayson, you have already given me so much joy. What more could you give me?"

"This." He extracted the small red velvet pouch and opened it, spilling the contents into her hands.

"It is so beautiful." She wiped at tears which pooled in the corners of her eyes.

"It was Mother's, and she received it from Father's mother on the occasion of their engagement. It is my wish to present it to you."

"I do not know what to say… except, thank you. It is the prettiest bracelet I have ever seen, and I will cherish it all my life." She held her wrist out and he secured it over her white gloved hand.

"Family, it is almost time to leave. Alex, you will stay upstairs with Lord and Lady Steinbright's grandchildren until your sister's nuptials." Lord Satterfield surveyed his little family. "Harding, my wife Anna always hoped you and my daughter would find each other at this point in your lives. I cannot help but think she has had a hand in this. She was wont to say this is the season for miracles, and renewal. I cannot help but feel grateful that God has been watching over my family."

The ballroom was the loveliest she could have ever imagined. Gold and white flocked wallpaper covered the walls. Brightly shining chandeliers hung from the ceiling. Large boughs of evergreens and mistletoe decorated with small silver bells framed the entrances and exits. A white arch, decorated with crystals, and a beautiful kissing bough made of evergreen foliage, mistletoe, and silver bells, stood in front of the platform where the orchestra sat playing.

This evening had been nothing short of magical. Susan's card had filled up quickly, and while her feet were a little tired, nothing could dampen her enthusiasm and her happiness. *Can this actually be the day I imagined?* She looked at her dress. The modiste had done a marvellous job of following the sketch she and Mama had created. Her dress fit like a glove, as if a fairy godmother had made it from the sketches and conversations that she and Mama had discussed all those years ago. Susan gently felt around her neck for the ruby and pearl necklace that had been her Mama's. She could feel her mother's presence. The music was festive and romantic. Susan and Grayson were just completing their second waltz when a tinkling bell sounded.

"Gentlemen, ladies, please honour our family and join us for a special Christmastide marriage between my daughter, Lady Susan Winslow and Earl Harding. Please gather around as we celebrate their union."

Susan did not remember seeing her little brother arrive, but he was standing next to her father. She felt as though she were in a dream of her own making, yet this was real. It was actually happening!

"Shall we?" She nodded and rested her hand on Grayson's proffered arm as he led her forward. Archbishop Nicholas came from behind the orchestra to a beautifully decorated altar which seemed to have appeared by magic.

Be happy, Susan. She heard her mother's voice again, and her heart filled with joy.

The ceremony was beyond any dream she could have imagined. Lady Harding had arranged everything to perfection. It was almost as if Mama had planned it herself. She became lost in thought, absorbed by all that had happened these past weeks.

"I do." Grayson's deep melodic voice beckoned her, bringing her back from her reverie—his soulful green eyes holding her captive.

"And do you, Lady Susan Deborah Winslow, take Grayson Daniel James Harding, the sixth Earl Harding, as your lawful husband? Do you promise to love, honour, and cherish him in sickness and in health, forsaking all others, so long as you both shall live?" Despite the Archbishop's sombre voice as he recited the vows, a peacefulness washed over Susan.

"I do," she said, smiling up at Grayson, sure her eyes must shine like the brightest stars.

"Then by the power vested in me, I now pronounce you husband and wife."

Grayson pulled her to him and kissed her, brushing her lips softly at first before he drew her closer for a deeper kiss. The Archbishop cleared his throat and Grayson broke the kiss.

"May I present Lord and Lady Harding?"

The audience clapped as the orchestra reappeared and began playing, their music low and lovely. The room grew quiet as Grayson lifted her hand and led her from the altar to the dance floor to celebrate their nuptials with a waltz, their wedding dance. Their happiness ignited the room, and other couples soon joined them, all gaily dancing to the waltz alongside Susan and her beloved husband. *I am so happy. Thank you, Mama.* She spoke to her mother with her heart.

"My dearest wife, is this the wedding you would have wished for?" Grayson eased her about the room, his arm holding her close. He drew her tighter against him and brushed his lips across hers, his eyes glistening.

"Oh, yes, husband. I am filled with a joy I did not know was possible." She took a breath, exhaling slowly, with her eyes closed and her smiling face upturned. "Your mother created Heaven on earth for us this day. I could never have imagined such a glorious wedding. I am filled with bliss. And, my dearest, what of you?"

"My love… how can you ask?" He gave her a tender kiss on the forehead. "No matter where we are, my home is forever where you are."

A loud tinkling of bells above them drew their attention to the largest and most beautiful kissing bough she had ever seen.

Gently brushing her lips, he whispered, "I love you, dearest Susan."

"And I love you, Grayson. I did not know that a reprobate earl could bring me such happiness beneath a bough of silver bells and mistletoe."

AFTERWORD

Please note: I wrote this book using historic British English spellings and grammar to better reflect the time period of the story. For example, I used favour instead of favor, parlour instead of parlor, marvellous instead of marvelous, and colour instead of color.

ACKNOWLEDGMENTS

There are always many people to thank when a book gets written. There are my friends who always cheer me on…EJ, Betty, Pat, Heather, Susan, and Lauren.

A great big 'thank you' goes to my team of readers who spent time and gave up evenings to help me smooth out the rough edges. I always appreciated your help.

And last *but never least*, my hero—my husband and best friend, Roger. He reads every one of my stories.

ABOUT THE AUTHOR

Anna St.Claire is a big believer that nothing is impossible if you believe in yourself. She sprinkles her stories with laughter, romance, mystery and lots of possibilities, adhering to the belief that goodness, lots of chocolate and love will win the day.

Anna is both an avid reader author of American and British historical romance. She and her husband live in Charlotte, North Carolina with their two dogs and often, their two beautiful granddaughters, who live nearby. Daughter, sister, wife, mother, and Mimi--all life roles that Anna St. Claire relishes and feels blessed to still enjoy. And she loves her pets - dogs and cats alike.

Anna relocated from New York to the Carolinas as a child. Her mother, a retired English, and History teacher, always encouraged Anna's interest in writing, after discovering short stories she would write in her spare time.

As a child, she loved mysteries and checked out every Encyclopedia Brown story that came into the school library. Before too long, her fascination with history and reading led her to her first historical romance--Margaret Mitchell's Gone With The Wind, now a treasured, but weathered book from being read multiple times. The day she discovered Kathleen Woodiwiss', books, Shanna and Ashes In The Wind, Anna became hooked. She read every historical romance that came her way and dreams of writing her own historical romances took seed.

Today, her focus is primarily on the Regency and Civil War eras, although Anna enjoys almost any period in American and British history. She would love to connect with any of her readers on her website - www.annastclaire.com, through email--annastclaireauthor@gmail.com, BookBub - www.-bookbub.com/profile/anna-st-claire,Twitter - @1AnnaSt-Claire, Facebook - https://www.facebook.com/authorannastclaire/ or on Amazon - https://www.amazon.com/Anna-St-Claire/e/B078WMRHHF?ref=.

ALSO BY ANNA ST. CLAIRE

Manufactured by Amazon.ca
Bolton, ON

20204084R00085